"Martha Jane Orlando is a talented storyteller with a gift for creating a cast of characters who are as winsome as they are wise. Orlando's new *Adventures in The Glade Series* opens with *Book One: Revenge!*, as ten-year-old Davy and the Old Ones come face-to-face with a pervasive darkness which threatens them all. Will good triumph over evil? Will the Chosen One, Reverend the Owl, Racer the Squirrel, and the rest of the beloved creatures of The Glade survive the chaos which has descended upon their sublime world? You'll turn these pages quickly as the tension builds and culminates in a suspenseful cliffhanger that will leave you eagerly anticipating Book Two of Martha Jane Orlando's *Adventures in The Glade Series.*"

– Michelle DeRusha, author,
Spiritual Misfit: A Memoir of Uneasy Faith and
50 Women Every Christian Should Know: Learning from Heroines of the Faith

"Welcome back to the magical, mystical world of The Glade! In her newest novel, *Revenge!*, Martha Jane Orlando weaves a spell-binding tale of family, friendships, and adventure. The story will enchant you and the ending? It will leave you breathless!"

– Mimi Moseley, author,
Arm Around Shoulder/Hand Over Mouth

"*Revenge!* takes Davy and his family back to The Glade and to yet another round of adventures. But, Cousin Ronnie has his heart set on nabbing the property that Grandpa Will left for Davy's step-father, Jim. He will stop at nothing to get the farm. Has he discovered that the Old Ones exist? If he has, what will he do to them? Davy's quest to protect his friends may not come to fruition and it may put him in danger. Will he succeed? Martha Orlando is a gifted storyteller and has used her pen to craft another story filled with intrigue, suspense, and of course, magic."

– Jennifer Barker, author,
Walking in the Spirit

ALSO BY MARTHA JANE ORLANDO

THE GLADE SERIES:

A Trip, A Tryst and a Terror

Children in the Garden

The Moment of Truth

REVENGE!

ADVENTURES IN THE GLADE | BOOK 1

MARTHA JANE ORLANDO

REVENGE!

ADVENTURES IN THE GLADE | BOOK 1

Martha Jane Orlando

Published November 2014
Little Creek Books
Imprint of Jan-Carol Publishing, Inc.

ISBN: 978-1-939289-53-7
Library of Congress Control Number: 2014957217

You may contact the publisher:
Jan-Carol Publishing, Inc.
PO Box 701 Johnson City, TN 37605
publisher@jancarolpublishing.com
jancarolpublishing.com

Revenge! is dedicated

in loving memory

to my father,

William Henry Murdy.

ACKNOWLEDGMENTS

My decision to begin a new series, *Adventures in The Glade*, to continue the stories of Davy, his family, and the Old Ones, was not made in a vacuum. I had encouragement from so many friends and fans who are all deserving of a big shout-out of appreciation for their love and support, but if I didn't feel as though God had his hands all over this novel, *Revenge!*, it would never have seen the light of day. He inspired every word and provided the best company on those long days of sitting at my computer, creating the book you now hold in your hands.

It is my honor and privilege to thank the following:

The awesome folks at Jan-Carol Publishing, Inc., whose skills and patience are much valued: Janie C. Jessee; Kasey Jones; Amy Frazier; Joy Martin; Tara Sizemore, and Tammy Robinson Smith.

Friends and fellow authors, Jennifer Barker, Michelle DeRusha, Mimi Moseley, and Lynne Watts for taking the time to read *Revenge!* and providing such thoughtful reviews.

My immediate family: You have always been there to give me love and inspiration.

My Facebook friends and fellow bloggers: You wrote reviews, promoted *The Glade Series* on your own pages, and were always there to give me a much needed word of reassurance.

My Kennesaw United Methodist Church family: Your prayers and support have provided me with peace and comfort during this writing journey.

All you delightful fans who purchased *The Glade Series* and begged for more, you are the best!

And, last, but definitely not least, my wonderful husband, Danny, my best friend and the love of my life. Your unfaltering support for my writing means the world to me! In the immortal words of Ralph Kramden: "Baby, you're the greatest!"

Letter to the Reader

I am thrilled to know you are holding the first book in the next Glade series, *Adventures in The Glade*, in your hands. If you have already read all three novels in *The Glade Series*, *A Trip, a Tryst and a Terror*, *Children in the Garden*, and *The Moment of Truth*, you are fully prepared to dive into *Revenge!*, as it is the continuing story of Davy, Racer, and all the Old Ones in The Glade.

If you haven't read the previous stories, I strongly suggest you do so before reading *Revenge!*. While I believe it is a novel which can stand independently on its own merits, you will be much more satisfied and intrigued if the previous novels are under your belt.

So, go ahead! Buy *Revenge!*, but don't crack the cover until you've experienced all the previous adventures, mystery and suspense in *The Glade Series* which lead up to this tale. You can order *The Glade Series* at my website: www.gladetrilogy.wix.com/theglade, and you can e-mail me with your comments, questions and suggestions at that very same site. Rest assured, I will respond to you promptly. I highly value your input, and am always glad to hear your opinions.

To those of you who have become loyal fans of *The Glade Series*, I salute you and thank you! For you who are new to this series, I welcome you, wholeheartedly, on board for a reading experience like no other. And, remember always, dear ones, as Racer would say, "It's all about love and grace." Amen, Racer. It is!

Love and blessings,
Martha Jane Orlando

Prologue

Ten-year-old Davy Murray detests the idea of spending the summer with his mother, Kate, step-father, Jim, and pesky sister, Anna at Grandpa Will's farm in the mountains. There is no television, no pool, no friends, and >gasp< no computer! Davy thinks his summer is ruined until he meets Grey (later known as Racer), the True Squirrel of the Old Ones, ancient creatures who reside in The Glade; creatures which only Davy can see and hear.

Through their adventures together, Davy grows close to the Old Ones and, miraculously, begins to appreciate his own family in a new and refreshing light. Kate and Jim are delighted with the boy's transformation, and prayerfully hope this kinder, gentler Davy will stay for good.

When it is discovered that Jim's devious cousin, Ronnie, is plotting to steal part of Grandpa Will's acreage in order to construct tourist cabins, the Old Ones are mortified. Ronnie is building on their mountain! If he succeeds, it will be the end of their lives in The Glade!

The Old Ones, with Davy's help, devise a plan to save their home. The Tomato Plan, as they call it, is a rousing success. Cousin Ronnie's plans are thwarted, and the Old Ones hold a special celebration in The Glade for Davy, his family, and their neighbors, Mr. and Mrs. Fairchild.

Revenge! continues the story...

Chapter 1

Best Birthday Present Ever!

It was twilight when the Hunters and the Fairchilds, along with Davy and Anna, descended the trail leading from The Glade to Willow Road at the foot of the mountain. They walked in companionable silence, each one reflecting on the marvelous events of that afternoon and early evening spent with the Old Ones. For the grown-ups, the memories now seemed more like a faraway dream floating languidly through their minds—a dream recalled only in feeling, not in substance. If it weren't for the garlands they all wore, they might have denied having dined and conversed with these mystical creatures at all. How outlandish and impossible it seemed to minds too long immersed in the practicalities of adulthood!

For Davy and Anna, though, the experience was as real and vibrant as the beating of their hearts. Anna had been entranced the moment she had laid eyes on the Old Ones, and had talked and danced and laughed with them as if she'd known them all her life. While watching his sister interacting with them, Davy wished that she could share his wondrous ability to see and hear the Old Ones whenever they were close at hand. By revealing themselves to his family, as well as to Mr. and Mrs. Fairchild, Davy knew the Old Ones had imparted a remarkably memorable gift to them all.

When they neared the bottom of the mountain and saw afresh the bulldozers and backhoes like hulking dinosaurs crouched at the base where they had been frantically abandoned just this morning, the sweet spell which clung to them dissipated as morning mist in the sunrise. "Man, oh, man," Jim said with a low whistle. "It sure didn't take them much time to do some damage here, did it?"

"You can say that again," Bob Fairchild agreed. "Wonder how the good Sheriff Peabody fared this afternoon with your cousin, Ronnie."

Jim scratched his head and chuckled. "You know, to tell you the truth, I haven't once thought about it since we entered The Glade. Looking at this mess here has a way of returning you to reality," he said, gesturing at the mangled forest.

"That had to be the most delicious food I ever put in my mouth," Susie Fairchild declared, oblivious to the men's conversation.

"I agree," said Kate, a soft smile playing on her lips. "It was enchanting, and it probably was enchanted. I doubt I'll ever enjoy my own cooking again."

"Yes, you will, Mom," Davy assured her. "It does wear off in time."

"Aha!" Mom exclaimed. "So, that's why you couldn't or wouldn't eat all of your lunch yesterday; you had just returned from a similar feast!" Davy nodded and flashed his mother a winning grin.

"All I know," said Anna sorrowfully, "is that Mary and I already miss the Old Ones. I wish we could have stayed the whole night!" She gave her doll a tight squeeze that threatened to crush both their necklaces.

"You'll see them again," said Davy, giving her a pat on the shoulder. "Remember, Racer promised, and Old Ones always keep their promises."

"But it's not fair," she proclaimed, her voice sliding into a whine. "You get to see them all the time and I don't." Davy hadn't heard that petulant tone in his sister's voice in almost a week. Maybe she had ingested too much of the chocolate mousse which Mrs. Hopper had, in a motherly fashion, warned her about, saying, "Only a wee bit, my love, only a wee bit or you'll upset your tummy."

Davy looked Anna squarely in the eyes, and said, "Life's not fair. That's all there is to it." The adults were understandably taken aback when they heard Davy utter these words, which bespoke wisdom far beyond his young years.

"And just where did you hear that?" Mom asked.

"Why, Reverend said it, of course," Davy answered.

"Of course," she echoed quietly, her eyes taking on a far-away look as if she were recalling a fond, but fading, memory.

"And I imagine," said Jim, regarding the boy affectionately, "that Reverend is right about a great many things."

"I wish he wasn't right about this one," Anna pouted.

"For your sake, Miss Priss, I wish he wasn't, either," Jim sympathized.

The small group finally reached their cars. Susie and Mom embraced, and Jim and Bob shook hands vigorously, as if each were leaving on a long trip and wouldn't see one another for weeks. At first, this seemed to Davy like rather odd behavior. When he saw tears shining in the eyes of Mrs. Fairchild and his mother, he suddenly understood: meeting the Old Ones had heightened everyone's emotions, just as it always did his. Racer had helped him to understand and value friendship in a true and meaningful way. Perhaps the grown-ups, too, realized with fresh clarity how precious the bond of friendship that had grown between them this week was. After all, they had just shared what Mom would always refer to later as The Miracle, and Davy knew those moments in The Glade touched them all deeply. The Old Ones had, indeed, affected everyone's hearts for the better.

Davy and Anna climbed into the back seat of Mom's car and fastened their seatbelts. When Jim and Mom joined them, Davy saw the ever-present tissue in her hand as she dabbed at her eyes and peered at her reflection in the visor mirror to wipe away any stray mascara. Actually, after all of the joyful tears that Mom had shed that day, there wasn't much left of it on her eyelashes. Davy decided she looked fine without it.

The ride home was fairly uneventful. Davy turned around several times to wave at the Fairchilds, who were following behind them. Anna was still quite out of sorts and finally admitted her stomach was hurting.

"We have some Pepto-Bismol at home, honey," Mom told her. "You can take some as soon as we get there."

"But it tastes so yucky!" she protested.

"What would be better?" Jim asked. "Taking the yucky medicine once, or having a bellyache all night?"

"Oh, all right," Anna conceded grumpily, "I'll take it."

"That's my girl," Mom said, turning around to give Anna a smile. "Maybe next time, you'll heed Mrs. Hopper's advice." Anna's only response was a low moan as she clutched Mary to her hurting abdomen. Davy decided to see if he could cheer her up.

"You know what I think is so neat, Anna?" he began. "Reverend said that Mary chose you, not the other way around. See, you're a Chosen One just like me!"

Anna managed a wan smile and hugged her doll more fiercely. "I just wish I felt better," she whispered.

"You will soon enough," Davy assured her. "You need to get better because, with all the crazy things that have happened this week, we haven't been able to go exploring like we planned. We could do it tomorrow if you're up to it."

Anna actually managed a real smile. "I'm sure I'll be okay by then," she said.

"Did I hear something about exploring?" Mom queried.

"Yes, Mom," Davy answered. "I promised Anna I'd take her exploring with me tomorrow. Is that okay with you?"

"Hmmm, let me think about that for a minute," she said. Davy noted the concern in his mother's voice, and hoped her answer would not be "no." Much to his relief, Jim decided to run interference.

"C'mon, Kate, say 'yes.' After what we experienced today, don't you think the kids are just as safe anywhere on the property as they are inside the house?"

Mom hesitated only a second or two before she relented. "You are absolutely right, Jim," she said. "How foolish of me not to think of that myself. I do believe Davy's friends will be their guardian angels anywhere they go, won't they, honey?" Mom looked back at him through the visor mirror and flashed him a radiant smile.

"Yes, I know they will!" Davy declared enthusiastically. Now he had the Old Ones to thank for yet another marvelous gift: he was free to roam anywhere he wished without inciting his mother's constant worry. The summer that he had thought couldn't possibly get any better, just did.

***

David and Sarah Murray were enjoying every moment of their retirement in Hawaii. They had fallen in love with the tropical paradise when David had been stationed there for a year, and vowed that one day they would return for good. Always frugal with their income, they had managed to save enough throughout the years to purchase a quaint bungalow near the beach, along which they would walk daily, enjoying the fresh ocean breezes and the continual song of the waves as they swept along the shoreline. Though they missed being able to see their two grandchildren, Davy and Anna, their daughter-in-law, Kate, sent them an e-mail at least once a week, updating them on the family's activities and frequently attaching photos of the children. They cherished these photos, and the best ones were printed, framed, and hung on walls or arranged on dressers and bedside tables. It gave them such comfort to see John's beautiful children growing up, and Davy looked more and more like his father every day.

"Except for his eyes," Sarah would always remark. "They're the same shade of brown as Kate's, aren't they, David?"

David would always chuckle at this, and remind her, "Green eyes are the rarest, dear. You know that. So lucky you are to have a green-eyed husband. You married one in a million, or there about."

"Yes, I *do* know that," Sarah would say with a smile. "I'm choosy and I chose the best."

Thursday afternoon after they had eaten lunch and had cleared and put away the dishes, Sarah seated herself at the computer to check her e-mail, which she had neglected to do for two days now and was certain it was piling up. She hoped she'd see one from Kate which included more photos of the grandchildren. While she was busy doing this, David settled down in his favorite easy chair, switched on the lamp, and began reading, his favorite pastime. He especially liked books on history, particularly military history, and was eager to plunge into his latest, *Don't Know Much About the Civil War.* He had only reached page three when he heard Sarah calling to him from the next room.

"Honey! Come quick! You have to see these great new photos Kate sent to us. She included pictures of the farmhouse Jim's grandfather owned. It's beautiful!"

David laid his book down and pushed himself up from the armchair. A twinge in his back warned him not to return to its inviting softness today, at least not without putting a brace around his middle. He shuffled in his worn, but cozy, house shoes to join his wife at the computer.

"Oh, good, here you are," Sarah said when David was standing at her shoulder. "I've looked at all of them twice already. Why don't you sit here and enjoy them while I make us some coffee?"

"That sounds good," David said, and eased himself down on the chair his wife had vacated. The first photos were of Davy and Anna. She was sitting on a lawn chair and he was standing behind her. He could see what he thought was a hen house in the background and rows of trees which, he assumed, was a modest apple orchard. The next photos were of Jim and a man he didn't recognize, leaning on their hoes in the middle of what appeared to be a vegetable garden of substantial size. *They'll certainly be eating healthy this summer. Wonder what all they're growing.* David continued to flip through the photos, astonished at the size of the oaks towering above the house, and marveling at the rolling mountains that surrounded the small valley. Something about this whole place seemed vaguely familiar to him, but he couldn't put his finger on it. Had he actually seen this mountainous view before, or was he simply confusing it with other photos he'd seen from time to time on the internet?

More photos of Anna and Davy. She was holding a rag doll, and he was patting the head of a beautiful golden retriever who, David knew, was named Maggie. Oh, what bright smiles the children wore! It made him grin just looking at their joyful faces, and he found himself wishing, not for the first time, that Sarah and he weren't long-distance grandparents. "Miss you, kiddos," David whispered and, with a sigh, continued on to the remaining photos. They were of the farmhouse. In a white-hot stab of recognition, memories, long buried, cut him to the quick. Past met the present like two trains colliding, and David was shaken to the core. One by one, like puzzle pieces perfectly matched, the picture came together. He knew what he had to do.

When Sarah entered the room, she was startled by the look on her husband's face. "David, what's wrong?" she asked anxiously as she placed his coffee mug on the computer desk. "You look like you've seen a ghost!"

He turned around to meet her gaze, his bright green eyes brimming with tears. "I have," he said.

***

That night as Davy lay on his cot, waiting for Mom to finish her nightly routine with Anna, who had perked up significantly after taking the medicine, Jim appeared on the porch with the now infamous survey map in hand. He switched on the light, causing Davy to blink furiously.

"Sorry about that, son," Jim apologized. "Your eyes will adjust in a moment, and then I'll show you something I've marked on this map that I thought would interest you." Davy sat up and Jim made himself comfortable on the edge of the cot. He unfolded the map and pointed to an "X" he had drawn on it. "See this here?" Jim asked. "This approximately marks the beginning of a beautiful trail that Anna and you might want to try out tomorrow. While it doesn't lead to the lake and a picnic table, it does take you to Big Bear Creek where, as I recall, there are some large boulders to sit on. It's definitely not as long as the hike we took last Saturday and should be perfectly manageable for Anna."

Davy's brow furrowed with unease. "Do you think I'll be able to find it?" he asked nervously, remembering how he would have strolled right past the side path to the lake if it hadn't been for Racer showing him the way.

"I certainly do," Jim assured him. "I'll point you across the meadow in the general direction. As you come closer to the woods, keep your eyes peeled for a wooden sign indicating the beginning of the trail. I made it myself when I was about your age, with Grandpa's help, of course."

"Really?" Davy remarked, his eyes wide. "And it's still there after all this time?"

At this, Jim threw his head back and guffawed heartily. Davy was uncertain as to what was so funny, but he found his stepdad's laughter contagious, and was soon laughing himself. "You know, son," Jim managed to say when he'd sufficiently regained his composure, "I don't think of myself as old, but to someone as young as yourself, I guess I could be labeled as ancient. Yes, it's still there. I saw it when Maggie and I walked the meadow the week before you got here. By the time we reached the trail, I knew she was too tired to attempt it, so we turned back around."

"Do you think Mom will let us take her camera?" Davy asked hopefully.

"Maybe," Jim said, "I suppose you'll have to ask her about that."

"Can I take my BB gun?"

Jim was caught off guard by this request, but quickly settled on a response. "I hate to tell you 'no,' but it's not a good idea, especially since Anna will be with you. Plus, without a carry bag for it, you'd get awfully tired of toting it anyway. Let's just save the gun for target practice for the time being."

Davy felt a shade disappointed in this, but he fully understood Jim's reasoning. After all, he was still new at shooting and, with Racer and the other Old Ones at the ready, he had no need for added protection. His backpack, heavy with their lunches, water bottles and, he hoped, the camera, would be enough to handle.

The two sat silently for the next few moments, and Davy noticed that Jim's eyes had taken on a dreamy gaze almost identical to Mom's earlier that day. "Jim, are you thinking about The Glade?"

Jim was startled. "How did you know?"

"Because Mom had that same look today when I mentioned Reverend," Davy answered.

"I see," said Jim. "Yes, today was quite out of the ordinary to say the least. Even though I know it happened, there's a part of me that finds it difficult to reconcile this fantastical experience with the logic I've applied to most things in my adult life. It truly gave me insight, though, as to why Grandpa often acted the way he did."

"What do you mean?" Davy wondered. "What kind of things did he do?"

"Oh, he was real careful about it, mind you," said Jim, "but, there were times I'd catch him talking to what I thought had to be himself since no one else was around, but now I know he was actually speaking to a living being. He'd also go off by himself on long walks only to return a few minutes before supper, and then receive a scolding from Grandma because he hadn't been around when this or that chore needed doing." Here Jim paused, his green eyes twinkling. "Grandpa would always give her a peck on the cheek, wash his hands, tell her how good the food smelled, and sit down at the table with his blue eyes full of joy. Grandma never stayed angry with him for more than a minute of two. 'It's those eyes of his,' she'd say, 'melted me the first time I saw them, and I guess they always will.'"

Davy smiled at this, but it faded as he entertained another thought. "I miss my grandparents," he sighed. "I wish they didn't live so far away. You were lucky to grow up with yours."

"Yes. Yes, I was," Jim affirmed. "I miss them both terribly—my mother, too. But I know one day we will all be together again, and I take great comfort in that."

Silence reigned between them once again. Davy felt an unexpected wave of weariness pass over him, and he leaned his head against Jim's broad shoulder. Touched yet again by his stepson's unfamiliar, but welcome, overtures, Jim put his arm around the boy and held him close, thanking God for this transformation and knowing, in his heart of hearts, that the Old Ones had led Davy in this blessed direction.

Davy stirred ever so slightly and, in a voice tainted with impending sleep, posed Jim a question. "Do you think if Anna and I ask them," he said, "that Mr. and Mrs. Fairchild would be our pretend grandparents for the summer?"

Jim was genuinely moved and surprised by Davy's sincere proposal. He cleared his throat several times before he dared to trust his voice. "Yes, Davy, I'm sure they would be thrilled. To tell the truth, I think they've already adopted you two as family. Asking would only be a formality, but it would be the right thing to do."

"Then I'll talk to Anna about it tomorrow. I'm sure she'll think it's a neat idea."

"What neat idea is this?" Mom asked, just catching this last snippet of conversation as she entered the porch.

Davy, with some effort, raised his head up from Jim's shoulder and lay back down on his pillow. Jim stood up and helped Mom straighten the covers. "You tell her, Davy," he said as he tucked the sheet and blanket at the foot of the cot.

"I was going to check with Anna tomorrow to see if she'd like us to ask Mr. and Mrs. Fairchild to be our grandparents for the summer," he told her.

"Why, Davy!" Mom exclaimed. "That is a wonderful idea! I can tell you right now they will lovingly and enthusiastically accept your offer. And speaking of grandparents," she paused to pull an e-mail from the back pocket of her jeans, "yours want to come visit us this summer while we're at the farm. Isn't that marvelous?"

Davy felt new life surging through his veins. He sat bolt upright in a flash. "You mean it? Really? They're going to visit us?" Then he stopped and stared at the paper in his mother's hand. "How did you get an e-mail here?" he asked, puzzled.

"Bob and Susie's computer," Mom answered. "That's how I sent Grandma Sarah and Grandpa David the photos I recently took of Anna, you, and the farmhouse, so they had an address to respond to. Susie gave this to me right before we began our walk to The Glade this afternoon."

"Hmm," said Jim, a bit perplexed by the news, "I wonder, why now?"

"What do you mean, honey?" Kate asked. "Why *not* now?"

"Well, it's just they didn't attend our wedding. Said it was too far and too expensive to travel from Hawaii," he remarked.

"Jim," said Kate, her voice low and soft, "John was their oldest son. Losing him broke their hearts. I think the thought of seeing me marry another man was simply too much for them at the time."

Jim sighed, "Makes sense to me. Hadn't thought about it that way, Kate."

"But when?" Davy interjected. "When will they be here?"

"They're hoping to be here in a week if they can get the flights they want," Mom announced, "and plan to stay at least through your birthday, Davy."

"But where will we put them up?" Jim asked worriedly.

"Oh, dear," said Mom, "I hadn't thought about that. I just now got around to reading the letter. That *is* a problem, isn't it?"

"Don't Mr. and Mrs. Fairchild have a guest room?" Davy asked. "Maybe, they could stay with them and I could have four grandparents for the first time in my life! That would be the best birthday present ever!"

"Looks to me like you've got your asking cut out for you tomorrow, son," Jim observed as he bent down to kiss Davy's forehead.

"Say your prayers, honey," Mom reminded his as she kissed him, too, and turned to go.

"Wait!" Davy called after them. "I need to say prayers with you tonight."

"You do? Why, how splendid!" Mom said delightedly as Jim and she returned to Davy's cot and joined hands.

"I'll say them tonight, if that's all right with you," he told them. They nodded in agreement. Davy closed his eyes, bowed his head, and prayed. "Heavenly Father, thank you for bringing my grandparents here to visit. Thank you for Mr. and Mrs. Fairchild; I hope they want to be our grandparents. And thank you for the Old Ones I love so much. Please bless all of my family and everyone I love. In Jesus' name, amen."

"Amen," Jim and Mom responded, pleased beyond measure at Davy's first attempt to lead prayer. They each gave him a hug, wished him a good night, and retreated to the interior of the house.

"Jim!" Davy called out before his stepdad disappeared through the doorway.

"Yes, Davy?"

"Do you have to set the alarm tonight? Racer might be stopping by, and I want to see him."

Jim faltered for a brief second, but then remembered the advice he'd given to Kate about the children's safety only hours before. "Consider it done," he said. "I think our troubles, at least for the present, are no longer a threat. May your amazing friends come and go as they please."

"Thanks, Jim," Davy said, and with that, he rolled over and slipped into a sleep filled only with blissful dreams of The Glade.

Chapter 2

Sheriff Peabody's Confrontation

The raucous jangling of the telephone awakened Davy the next morning. He rubbed his eyes sleepily and wondered what time it was, though by the yet dim light in the sky, he guessed it was fairly early. He heard Jim conversing with the caller, and curiosity got the better of him. Davy threw back his covers, bounced off his cot, and trotted to the kitchen where he noticed the clock said 7:00. This was the earliest he had gotten up, of his own free will, all summer long. Davy briefly entertained the thought of lying down again, but when he recalled that Anna and he were going exploring today, he found he was too excited to even contemplate falling back asleep.

Jim was standing at the phone, receiver in one hand and his first cup of coffee in the other. He seemed to be doing more listening than talking, so Davy couldn't identify the caller. He headed down the hall toward the bathroom and saw Mom, still in her pajamas and robe, emerge from it. "My, you're up early today," she said, stifling a yawn. "Did the phone wake you up, too?"

"Yes, it did," he said. "Who would call us so early?"

"I have no idea, but I'm about the find out. Hmmm, that coffee sure smells delicious this morning!"

Mom continued down the hall to the kitchen, and Davy slipped into the bathroom. In the mirror, he noticed his shiner had practically disappeared, no doubt another perk from being around the Old Ones, but his thick and wavy brown hair was tousled and out of control. He wet his comb and tried to tame his locks into an acceptable shape. While this exercise was successful, he decided it was high time to get it cut. He had kept it long on purpose, he noted regretfully, just because Jim's was a close-cropped, military style. Davy no longer felt the urge to be contrary or confrontational. *Everything has changed, and everything is for the better.* He decided to ask Jim to give him a buzz cut that very morning before Anna and he set out on their adventure. By the time Davy reentered the kitchen, Jim was off the phone and sitting at the table with Mom.

"Who was that on the phone?" he asked brightly as he walked to the pantry in search of cereal.

"It was Sheriff Peabody," Jim answered. "He asked if he could stop by this morning and fill us in on what happened with Ronnie yesterday. Get your breakfast and I'll give you a preview."

Davy hastily grabbed the Cheerios and milk while Mom washed off some blueberries for him, and then put a bowl, spoon and napkin at his seat. When they were both back in their places, Jim recounted the mostly one-sided conversation he had had with the sheriff.

"It turns out Peabody's staff encountered some problems trying to download those photos to the computer. While they were preoccupied with that issue, the sheriff got a call about a domestic disturbance which took him away from the office for the remainder of the afternoon." Jim paused a moment to sip his coffee. "By the time he returned, the problem had been solved, and even though he was due to be off his shift, he didn't want to pass this peculiar case onto one of his deputies since he had, as he put it, a 'rare investment' in this investigation."

"Wonder what he could have been referring to," Mom said with a knowing smile.

"Racer and Cleverhands, Mom. You know that!" Davy exclaimed, and smiled as he recalled how their instantaneous appearance on that very table the day before had so shocked the good sheriff that he had fallen off the bench.

"Anyway," Jim continued, "he drove out to Ronnie's home, which he called a log cabin mansion with a view any mountain lover would pay dearly for. Since he didn't want Ronnie to see them right away, he left the phone and charger in the patrol car, and that's all I know so far."

"I can't wait to hear the rest of the story!" Mom said excitedly. "Oh, dear, I'd better get cleaned up and dressed before he gets here." She jumped up and made a beeline for the bathroom. Within ten seconds, Davy could hear the water running.

"And, you need to get dressed as soon as you finish your cereal, Davy," Jim said. "I'm going to rouse Anna, as I'm sure she's going to want to hear this tale, too." As Jim made his way up the loft ladder, Davy gobbled down the last bites of his cereal as quickly as he could and cleared his place. He then ran full-tilt to the porch to change his clothes. He had just tied the last shoelace of his sneakers when he heard Racer's charming voice at the porch door.

"Are you going to let me in, Davy, or do I have to stand here all day?" he quipped, shining his lopsided smile, which had become so endearing to the boy.

"Racer! I'm so glad you're here!" Davy shouted, relieved now that he no longer had to hide his friend from his family. He opened the door for the squirrel, and was greeted with a ticklish peck on the cheek.

"Aren't you always glad when I'm here?" Racer teased.

"Of course, I am," Davy asserted. "It's just that Sheriff Peabody is on his way over here now to tell us what happened yesterday when he returned Ronnie's phone.

"Oh, this should be a good one. I feel it in my bones!" Racer said, rubbing his paws together in anticipatory glee. "I hope the sheriff gave him the what for!"

"Me, too," Davy agreed. "And, after we hear his story, Anna and I are going to exploring down the trail on the other side of the meadow. Can you come with us?"

"Is there a picnic involved?" Racer asked, licking his chops and giving the boy a wink.

"Yes, complete with pickles," he answered, knowing in his heart his friend would gladly tag along even if food wasn't included in the day's excursion.

"Excellent!" Racer said, and then suggested, "Why don't we start fixing the picnic while we're waiting for the sheriff? I'll supervise, if that's agreeable to you."

"Fine with me," Davy assured him. "I don't have much experience in picnic packing."

"After today, you will," Racer told him as he strutted toward the kitchen, his gleaming white chest puffed with pride. "I'm a premiere picnic packer, my child. No brag, just fact." Davy found this posture immensely amusing, and was so relieved he could laugh out loud at seemingly nothing, and no one would think he'd lost his marbles.

When they reached the kitchen, Anna was seated at the table eating her breakfast. She appeared to have fully recovered from yesterday's unfortunate ailment. "How are you feeling today?" Davy asked as he opened the refrigerator door.

"Much better," she said, "and I can't wait to go exploring. Are you making our lunches?"

"I'm going to try," he told her. "Anything special you want me to pack for you?"

Anna wrinkled her nose and made a sour face. "Anything's fine," she stated, "as long as it's not chocolate."

"Ahhh," Racer observed, "so your sister *did* have too much of that mousse yesterday, just as Mrs. Racer feared. I'm afraid it will be a good long while before Anna will crave any chocolate in her diet."

Davy found the pickle jar and put it on the table while Racer perused the contents of the fridge. "It looks like we have sliced turkey and ham!" he exclaimed with delight. "I'll take one of each, light on the mustard, heavy on the mayo. Oh, my, the grapes look marvelous, too. Let's wash a bunch of those, shall we? I'd love to take some blueberries, but it looks like you're running low, so I'll spare your mother. And what's this? Dare I trust my eyes? How I adore devilled eggs! We must pack some of those!"

Racer prattled on while Davy located the plastic wrap, sandwich bags, and bread, and spread them out on the long table beneath the kitchen windows. He then retrieved the items that the squirrel had indicated were crucial to a successful picnic. Once he had everything displayed, Racer coached him every step of the way, from how much mayonnaise he desired on his sandwich to the best way to wrap devilled eggs. By the time Mom returned to the kitchen, showered, dressed, and ready for her second cup of coffee, Davy was just gathering up what seemed like a mountain of sandwiches. He placed them back in the fridge so they would stay chilled until it was time to go.

"Don't tell me you made your own picnic lunch?" Mom asked, incredulous.

"Well, sort of," Davy admitted. "I had some help."

"I see," said Mom with a meaningful smile. "That would explain why you made so many sandwiches for two small people. And Davy," she added, "don't forget to pack some almonds."

"Oh, boy!" Racer exclaimed. "I nearly forgot about those. Your mother is one smart cookie. Tell her I give my most gracious thanks for her generosity."

"Racer says 'thanks,' Mom."

"You're very welcome, Racer," she said politely, "wherever you are." She poured herself another cup of coffee and prepped the machine for a fresh pot in light of Sheriff Peabody's impending visit. Anna had returned to the loft to get dressed, and Jim had gone to the hen house to feed the chickens and gather the eggs. Davy left Racer contentedly munching almonds on the pantry counter while he returned to the porch to retrieve his backpack and the water bottles. It was then he noticed Maggie still sleeping on her bed. *That's strange. Maggie always gets up to get her food when she hears Jim in the morning.* Feeling apprehensive, Davy approached her and knelt by her side to gently stroke her fur. Her eyes fluttered open briefly and, when she saw him, her tail thumped once, but then, lay motionless.

"Racer!" Davy hollered, panic in his voice. "Come quick! It's Maggie!"

The squirrel was beside him in a flash. Immediately, he understood why the boy had sounded so frantic. "Maggie?" he spoke gently to the old dog. "Aren't you feeling well today?"

"Not too well, I must admit," she whined weakly. "Nothing a little nap won't cure."

"Don't you want your breakfast?" Davy asked, tears welling up in his eyes as he continued to run a soothing hand along her back.

"Not now," she told him, "but if you fill my bowl, I'll get to it later."

"How about going outside?" Racer inquired.

"Jim took me out early," she said, and heaved a sigh. "Don't worry, I'm fine; just tired."

"Tell you what, Maggie," the squirrel said as he lovingly scratched her behind the ears, "we'll bring your food and water in here so you won't have to go far when you do feel like eating."

"That would be nice," she said in a voice so low they almost couldn't hear her. She closed her eyes again and was dozing away within the minute.

"Is she going to be okay?" Davy asked in a quavering voice.

Racer's face wore the most solemn expression the boy had yet seen. "To be honest, my child, I'm not sure. It's possible that Maggie got into some forbidden food while all of you were at The Glade yesterday, and that has made her unwell. We'll just have to wait and see how she feels when she wakes up."

"Maybe we shouldn't go exploring today after all," Davy suggested. "Maybe we should stay right here with Maggie."

"She wouldn't want you to do that, Davy," Racer assured him. "She'd feel terrible if she found out you skipped a big adventure just because she is under the weather. Besides, you can let Jim and your mother know how she's acting this morning, and I'm sure they'll keep a watchful eye on her for you."

"I suppose you're right," Davy acknowledged reluctantly. He bent over and lightly held his ear to Maggie's ribcage. He could hear her heart beating; it sounded steady and strong, which did much to alleviate his fears. Racer did the exact same thing.

"I'd say her ticker is in fine shape for her age," he declared happily. "I'll bet you dollars to donuts she simply ate something she shouldn't have and is too embarrassed to confess. So put a smile on that face of yours, child, and let's go back to the kitchen. I hear the sheriff's patrol car in the distance!"

***

When they were all seated at the kitchen table, the adults with fresh cups of coffee, and Anna and Davy thrilled beyond words to be sipping the sodas with which Sheriff Eric Peabody had surprised them, the sheriff handed Jim a large manila envelope. "This is your copy of the original survey map we got off Mr. Carson's cell phone. I have another set in my office and am keeping a second at my home just for security purposes while I'm looking into all this. I'd put this in Bob Fairchild's safe as soon as you get the chance."

"You don't have to tell me twice, Sheriff Peabody," Jim said as he accepted the envelope. "I'll go down there as soon as we've wrapped things up here."

"Sounds good, but please, call me Eric," he said with a friendly smile, and turning to Davy, he added, "Now, Davy, before I start telling this story, can you assure me I won't be seeing any unusual visitors today?"

Racer, who had returned to the pantry to pilfer more almonds, laughed heartily. "No, sir," Davy answered. "They only become visible when there is a really, *really* good reason."

"Glad to hear it," Eric said, noticeably relieved. He took a swig of his coffee and began his story.

***

When Sheriff Eric Peabody's patrol car negotiated the last steep curve in the road that led to the Carson home, his breath was duly taken away. It was the largest, grandest log structure he had ever seen in these hills. It boasted two stories, floor to ceiling windows, two enormous stone chimneys, a wrap-around porch on the first level, and screened-in decks on the second. Its colossal presence dwarfed everything around it, including the mountain upon which it had been built. Slowly, Eric eased the car along the gravel drive and parked it a few paces from the porch stairs. Not wishing to show his hand yet, he hid the cell phone and charger in his glove box, exited the car, and strode toward the front door. Before his foot hit the second stair, the door flung wide, and there stood Ronnie Carson wearing his best Cheshire cat grin.

"Welcome, Sheriff Peabody. Such a pleasure, such a pleasure. The missus and I hoped you'd have the time to stop by today. Come on in and make yourself at home," he insisted in a tone that Eric thought was a bit too sugarcoated to be sincere.

As he climbed the stairs, Eric noticed that Ronnie's right hand was wrapped with gauze. "Guess we won't be shaking hands today, Mr. Carson," he observed. "What happened?"

"Just a scratch, just a scratch," Ronnie insisted. "It ain't nothing to fret over."

"With all due respect, sir," Eric said, "that seems an awfully large bandage for something that's just a scratch." Ronnie didn't answer. He simply ushered the sheriff through the door and invited him to sit on a plush sofa by one of the two gigantic fireplaces the home boasted. When he sat down, Eric had to admit it was one of the most agreeable couches he had ever had the privilege to enjoy. He laid his hat beside him and pulled out his trusty notebook while Ronnie settled himself into an equally luxurious wing-tipped chair. At that moment, Betty Rae bustled in with a tray of mini-pizza bagels and placed them on the spacious coffee table shared by the couch and chair where each man was seated.

"I have some fresh-brewed iced tea, Sheriff. Would you care for some?" she asked, acting a bit too coy and flirtatious for Eric's comfort.

"Yes, ma'am," he responded, standing up as he had always been taught to do when a woman entered the room. "I'm assuming it's sweetened?"

"We're in the South, honey," she reminded him. "There isn't anything but." Betty Rae flounced away and returned briskly with a pitcher of tea and ice-filled glasses. "Now, I'll leave you two boys alone to talk your business. I'll be in the kitchen if you need anything. Just give me a holler." After batting her heavily made-up eyes at Eric, Betty Rae retreated, thankfully, as far as he was concerned, from the scene. As much as he dreaded it, if Eric needed her to corroborate any evidence Ronnie might throw his way, he would, indeed, have to "holler." He hoped it wouldn't come to that. Ronnie reached for the mini-bagels and popped two at once into his mouth, motioning for Eric to do the same. The sheriff poured himself a glass of tea and helped himself to one of the appetizers. As he hadn't eaten much all day and was dealing with a growling stomach, he was particular disappointed to discover they tasted just as he had imagined—like cardboard. He managed to chew and swallow what he now regretted eating, and then got down to the matter at hand.

"Mr. Carson," he began.

"Call me Ronnie, please, Sheriff. We're all friends here," he said, devouring three more mini-bagels.

"Yes, sir." Eric cleared his throat and took a swallow of his tea, which he was relieved to find delectable in comparison to the bland taste of the bagel. He found himself wishing he had some of Kate Hunter's cookies right about now. "Ronnie," he began, leaning forward on the couch so as not to become too relaxed, "let's review what happened at the work site this morning. I have some notes here from my assistant, and I need to clarify a few things with you. If you don't mind, I'd like you to recount the facts exactly as you recall them."

Ronnie flinched almost imperceptibly, but Eric, with his trained eye, didn't miss a move. "Yes, yes, I'll do the best I can," Ronnie answered, shoving two more of the unpalatable pizza bites into his mouth. "You see," he claimed, talking with his mouth full, "I was on my own property, which I had planned to develop for some time now, and had all the workers engaged in exactly what they were supposed to be doing. You do know I own the mountain adjacent to this one as well?"

"I know those are your cabins, yes," Eric asserted.

"Well, sir, much to my surprise and alarm, my cousin, Jim Hunter, the one I reported to your very competent assistant, Connie, showed up with his friend and stepson in tow and proceeded to accuse me of all kinds of unlawful behaviors. I tried to assure him that he was mistaken about the ownership of the property. It may have belonged to my dear Great-great-uncle Will, God rest his soul, at one point, but no longer. The survey I obtained from the public records office speaks for itself."

"And I suppose you also have the deed of sale which confirms the property belongs to you, am I right?" Eric asked calmly, thinking this question might turn the heat up on Ronnie.

"The deed? The deed?" Ronnie repeated with only the merest trace of nervousness in his voice. "Of course I have the deed. Well, not here at the house. I'd have to pick it up from my attorney, who reviewed it and finally gave me the go-ahead for the construction project. I'll do that first thing Monday morning and have it filed in the public records office so you can examine it there."

"Very good. I'll do just that," said Eric, jotting it down in his notebook. "Now, what's this about the physical assault perpetrated against you by Mr. Hunter? Can you tell me more about it?"

Here Ronnie paused to take a long swallow of iced tea and then wiped his mouth with the back of his uninjured hand. "Well, sir," he began, "Jim grabbed me by my shirt and slammed me against the side of the trailer where he pinned me and, I hate to say it, him being my cousin and all, threatened to kill me. Then he threw me to the ground."

"He threatened to kill you?" Eric asked, quickly flipping back to the notes he had taken of Jim's testimony earlier in the day. "What did he say exactly?"

"Right in my face, I tell you, right in my face, Jim kept insisting how the property was his and he was going to take it back if it was the last thing he did. Well, I wasn't about to put up with that nonsense, so I said, 'over my dead body.' That's when he said, 'don't tempt me.' I don't know about you, Sheriff, but I'd call that a threat." Ronnie downed the rest of his iced tea and refilled his glass.

Eric scribbled down information before he continued. "Mr. Carson, I mean, Ronnie, as you've probably conjectured, I paid Mr. Hunter a visit as soon as I got the report from my office. He did admit to saying the statement you quoted, and conceded that his choice of words could have been better."

"Dang right, they could have," Ronnie said adamantly, throwing down another bagel.

"However," Eric continued, "his response seemed more of a knee-jerk reaction to your statement. I wouldn't necessarily consider it a threat."

Ronnie's mouth dropped open in disbelief. "Not a threat?" he asked. "How can you think that? Oh, unless you think Jim is off his rocker more than *I* think he is. He sure came unhinged, I'll tell you. Why, Sheriff, I do believe that if he'd had his gun on him, he would've shot me right there."

"Mr. Hunter seemed quite sane when I spoke to him," Eric informed Ronnie. "He insisted that the property in question belongs to him. Why do you think he feels that strongly about it if it, as you allege, belongs to you?"

"Allege? I don't allege nothin'!" Ronnie pounded his fist on the table for emphasis. "I own the damn property, free and clear, and I ain't havin' that fool of a cousin of mine dictating what I can and can't do with it. In fact, I'd like to get a restraining order against him. Yes! That's what I want, a restraining order! I'm sure you can arrange that now, can't you?"

Eric regarded him sternly. "I could," he said slowly, as if he was mulling over alternative actions in his mind, "but I'm not going to because I don't think Mr. Hunter poses any danger to you. Excuse me for a moment, Ronnie. I've left something of importance in the car which might be of interest to you. I'll be right back."

Eric stood up abruptly and showed himself to the door. Ronnie sat as if he were glued to his chair, astonished by the answer the sheriff had given, and becoming hotter under the collar with each passing moment. "What the hell kind of sheriff are you, Peabody, not doin' right by folks?" he muttered under his breath. "You better be careful going against me like that. I can make or break elections in this county."

When Eric reached the car, he removed the cell phone and charger from his glove box and slipped them into his pocket. He returned as promptly as promised, but didn't reclaim his seat on the sofa. Instead, he stood toweringly, only two feet away from Ronnie, which unnerved the man greatly. Eric thought he detected, for the first time, a hint of real apprehension in Ronnie's eyes. He reached into his pocket and produced the two items which, only that morning, Ronnie had feared were gone forever. Before he could catch himself, he blurted out the truth, something with which he was rarely familiar. "It's my cell phone! I've been looking all over for that blasted thing. Where did you find it?"

"Where I found it or how I, rather, came by it is of no consequence," Eric told him firmly. "What is important is that it's now in the hands of the rightful owner." He handed the phone and charger to Ronnie, picked up his hat off the couch, and turned as if he was heading out for good. Unexpectedly, he spun around and fixed Ronnie with a steely gaze which made the man cringe inside. "Please convey my thanks to Mrs. Carson for the tea and snacks. It was thoughtful of her. Oh, and Ronnie," he added, "just as I advised Mr. Hunter that I would have to arrest him should he attack you again, I will have to do the same to you if I hear of you trespassing on his land. By the way, the photos were superb."

With that parting comment, Eric donned his hat and walked out the door, leaving a stunned and bitter Ronnie in his wake.

Chapter 3

A Milestone for Mom

"I wish I'd had a camera to catch the look on your cousin's face when I mentioned the photos," Eric confessed. "It was priceless!"

"And if only I could have been a fly on the wall," Jim chuckled, "I would have relished every minute. You nailed him good, Eric, no doubt about it."

Racer was laughing so hard by the story's conclusion, he nearly rolled off the pantry counter. "That lousy lout got what was coming to him!" he exclaimed when he finally caught his breath. "Well done, Eric, my boy. Well done!"

"Sheriff Peabody?" Davy spoke up, deciding to pass along the squirrel's accolades. "Racer says it was a job well done." Eric almost choked on his last sip of coffee, and his eyes darted furtively around the room as if they could detect where the creature was hiding. "Don't worry," Davy assured him. "He's here, but, as I said before, you won't see him. He really enjoyed your story."

"He did?" Eric looked straight at the boy, and the edginess he felt just seconds ago vanished completely.

"Yes," said Davy. "He laughed so much he almost fell off the counter!"

"I wonder which counter I'll have to sanitize," Mom said in an exaggerated tone with a smile to match.

"Good one, Kate," Racer called good-naturedly. "Why don't you check the almond supply?"

Mom turned to Davy and said, "Am I on the money here by guessing Racer is once again helping himself to the almonds?"

"You got it, Mom," he confirmed with a grin, but was left to wonder if she had truly heard Racer as she had Prancer just days before. He decided that, when the moment presented itself, he would have to ask in order to set his mind at ease.

Impulsively, Anna jumped up and dashed into the pantry. "I love you, Racer," she declared to the empty counter. "Mary does, too. She told me so." She blew a kiss into the air and skipped back to the table. Racer, touched deeply by the little girl's candor, wiped away an unforeseen tear. He realized, after all the years he'd spent only with Will, how much he had missed being around a family, one that could share in his presence even though they could only occasionally see and hear him. It drained so much of his spirit to physically display himself, and a rejuvenating return to The Glade was ever eminent when he did so. Having a family who understood, and precious Davy to convey his messages, meant the world to Racer.

"Thank you, my Lord and Creator," he breathed in prayer. "Thank you for everything, past and present. I am grateful beyond words."

"Well, Jim, Kate," Eric said as he stood up to leave, "I don't think you have anything to worry about at the present time as far as Ronnie is concerned, but I'm not through with this investigation yet. It's obvious he's had help with this little scheme, and I'm determined to get to the bottom of it."

"That's good news, Eric." Jim smiled and shook the sheriff's hand. "You'll keep us posted, won't you?"

"Sure thing," Eric said. "Thanks for the coffee, Kate. It was mighty good."

"Thanks for the sodas!" Davy and Anna said in unison.

"You're very welcome," Eric said, tipping his hat toward them, which made them giggle. "You two take care and stay out of trouble. And Davy, don't let that Racer get you into more mischief, y'hear? Bye, Racer!"

Everyone laughed at Eric's farewell to Racer, gratified to know the affable sheriff was finally comfortable in the presence of an Old One. Once again, Jim escorted Eric to his patrol car. "So, you really think this has taken the wind out of Ronnie's sails for a while?"

"Yes, I do," Eric responded. "Still, I'd keep my eyes peeled and my ear to the ground when it comes to your cousin. He's a champion liar and treacherous to boot."

"Advice taken," Jim said. "Thanks for everything, Eric. Oh, and just to not leave any stone unturned, could you check out the land records at the courthouse when you get a chance? I think Ronnie's bluffing, but I'd like to know for sure."

"You bet, Jim. I'll be there Monday afternoon. You can count on it," Eric said as he got into his car and put his keys into the ignition. The engine roared to life and, with a final wave, Eric sped up the gravel road faster than Jim thought was even possible.

Davy and Anna downed the remainder of their sodas and scurried to the bathroom, on Mom's orders, to brush their teeth. As soon as he was finished, Davy returned to the kitchen and began loading their lunches into his backpack. Mom was filling the water bottles at the sink. "I made Anna wear her jeans today with a belt so she can be responsible for own water. Davy, you have enough to carry."

"Don't forget these, Davy," Racer said, tossing a baggie full of almonds in his direction. Davy caught it deftly and stuffed it into his pack. He couldn't wait for this adventure to begin, and wondered what was taking Anna so long to get ready. Just then, Maggie, moving lethargically, but with a reassuring sparkle in her eyes, entered the kitchen.

"Look, Mom!" Davy shouted with delight. "It's Maggie! She must be feeling better."

"Oh, honey, that's wonderful!" Mom said, ceasing her activity at the sink to give the dog an affectionate pat.

Davy threw his arms around Maggie's warm, silky neck, and she leaned into him, almost toppling him over with her weight. "Yes, Davy, I'm feeling much better, but I made rather a mess out on the porch, I'm afraid."

"Oh, Maggie, so you *did* eat something you shouldn't have," he groaned.

The sweet dog hung her head in shame. "What was left of Anna's grilled cheese sandwich was calling from the garbage can and I simply could not resist," she admitted. "I won't do it again, honestly, because I never want to endure a stomach ache like that one ever again. Can you forgive me, Davy, for being so impulsive and thoughtless?"

"Of course I can, Maggie," he said, hugging her lovingly. "I'm just so glad you're better. I was so worried about you."

"As was I, dear girl," Racer told her, hopping down from the counter to scratch her ears in exactly the way she liked. "It's a tremendous relief to see you up and about. Do you understand now why I wouldn't share my food with you the other day?"

"Yes, Racer, I do," she said. "I know it's because you love me and want only the best for me. You have since I was a mere pup."

"You're right about that," he told her. "I've felt nothing but love for you from the day Will brought you home."

"And I've always loved you, too," Maggie said, and gave Racer's fur a wrong-way lick, as was her habit.

Just then, Jim came in through the kitchen door and smiled broadly when he saw the revived Maggie wrapped in Davy's arms.

"Well, well, if this isn't a sight for sore eyes," he declared. "I thought we'd be taking a trip to the vet today, but it looks like that won't be necessary." He approached the dog and, unbeknownst to him, took over the ear-scratching job Racer had been doing.

"It was Anna's leftover grilled cheese that made her sick," Davy explained. "I guess I should go clean up the mess on the porch."

"Grab some paper towels and a wet sponge, and I'll help you," Jim offered, not questioning how Davy knew the cause of the dog's illness as he assumed, since Racer was present, she had told him herself. Davy hurried to gather the things Jim requested and, when he turned around, Anna was standing in front of Mom holding Mary and a colorful scarf that Mom had given her to play dress-up.

"Do you think we could make a sling out of this so I can carry Mary on my back?" she inquired. "I don't want to leave her at home, but I know I'll get tired if I carry her in my arms, and I don't want to ask Davy to help me out. He already has the pack." Davy flashed his sister an appreciative grin, pulled gently on a braid as Jim often did, and headed for the porch to help eradicate the undesirable consequence of Maggie's indiscretion.

"I'm sure we can," Mom said. "Let's get this water bottle on your belt first and then I'll see what I can do for Mary."

When Jim and Davy arrived on the scene, the mess Maggie had made was greater than either of them had imagined. "Run back for some more towels, Davy," Jim instructed, "and, ask your mother for a garbage bag, too. I'll get moving on this." Davy did as Jim asked and returned to the porch as quickly as he could. He handed two towels to his stepdad and opened the garbage bag to receive the soiled ones. He really wanted to get down on his hands and knees and help, but even from a fair distance, the stench of Maggie's leavings was enough to turn his stomach.

"Jim, I can't get any closer," Davy said, holding his nose. "I can't handle the smell."

"You'll be able to one day," Jim assured him. "I had to get used to doing all kinds of unsavory chores when I was in the Marines. By the way, are you still intent on enlisting when you're old enough?"

"I wouldn't do anything else," Davy said proudly, realizing that, although he had previously wanted to only because of his father's military service, Jim had also bolstered his resolve.

Jim sopped up the last of the stinky mess, threw the towels in the garbage bag, and began sponging the floor. "That's good to hear," he said to Davy. "It's not easy at times, but I wouldn't trade one minute of my experiences, good or bad." He tossed the rancid sponge into the trash bag and dried the floor with the remaining towels. "One thing I can guarantee you, son. If nothing else, the military will make a man out of you, and that's the honest truth."

Jim tied up the bag and headed back to the kitchen with Davy following a few paces behind in an attempt to avoid the unpleasant odor. When they got there, Davy was gratified to discover that Mom had been successful in making a sling for Mary who was now cradled snugly in place and unlikely to be a burden to either Anna or him during today's trek.

"Yuck!" Anna exclaimed as Jim passed by her. "What's that smell?"

"Maggie's accident," Jim replied as he headed for the door. "I'm taking it to the outdoor can right now. Kate, I think we're going to have to get a better trash can for the indoors, preferably one with a secure lid."

Mom wrinkled her nose in distaste, too, as she caught a whiff of the odor. "Good idea," she called after him.

"Look, Davy," Anna said, pointing to her back. "See how I'm going to carry Mary today? Isn't it neat?"

"Yes, it is," he told her. "Are you all set to go?"

"Yes, yes! Let's go right now."

"Not so fast, you two," Mom cautioned. "Wait until Jim comes back. We need to remind you of a few things."

Davy and Anna reluctantly took their seats at the table while Racer helped himself to more almonds before hopping up on the bench beside Davy. "Tell them I'm coming along," the squirrel advised him. "They'll worry a lot less, don't you think?" Davy nodded and patted his friend's back in thanks.

When Jim arrived a few moments later, he headed straight for the kitchen sink to scrub his hands. "Whew, Maggie," he said, addressing the dog who was dozing underneath the table. "Let's watch what we eat in the future, okay?" In response, she thumped her tail twice on the floor.

"I think she's learned her lesson," Davy offered, reaching down to pat her.

"Yes, I have," she mumbled groggily. "There's no need for a different garbage can. I'll behave myself from now on."

"Mom, Jim, don't waste money on a new can," Davy said. "Maggie's promised to stick to her diet."

"Has she, now?" Mom inquired, exchanging knowing looks with Jim.

"Yes," he confirmed, "and you won't need to worry about us today because Racer is coming with us."

"For the whole time?" Anna asked excitedly.

"Yup, the whole time," Davy answered.

Jim, drying his hands on a dishtowel, focused on both children. "I'm glad to hear it," he said. "I know that Racer will take good care of you and return you safely home, or come fetch us should something happen where you can't make it back on your own. Still, there are a few words of advice, simple actually, that your mother and I want to give you before you go exploring the trail."

"Number one," Mom began, "you need to make sure to sip your water as you walk along. It's supposed to get fairly hot today, and you could find that you're dehydrated before you even realize it. That would *not* be a good thing."

"And," Jim added, "watch your footing. The trail I'm sending you on is fairly smooth, but you should always be mindful where you are stepping. That goes for the meadow, too."

"I'll negotiate it all, Jim," Racer declared. "Don't you fret about that!"

"Racer says he'll help us," Davy told them. "He's probably gone on enough walks with Grandpa Will, and all those before him, to know what we humans need, don't you think?"

Mom sighed and shook her head, a wan smile on her face. "I know Racer will help you, honey, but everything is all so different here. It's difficult for me to adjust to the changes so quickly," she admitted. "Why, just yesterday we were graciously invited to experience The Miracle, and now the children I've watched so closely and protected for all these years, I'm allowing to wander freely because I, without knowing why, trust Racer and the Old Ones to look out for my babies no matter where they are."

Jim approached her and placed an arm around her shoulders. "I think it's called 'walking by faith,' Kate," he reassured her. "Let them go and lay the worries to rest."

"All right," she acquiesced. "I'll try."

"Do you have everything you need, kids?" Jim asked.

"The camera!" Davy remembered suddenly. "Mom, is it okay with you if we take it along?"

"As long as you promise to be ever so careful with it," she said. "It's right there on the sideboard." Davy hustled over to get it, and Mom helped him hook the case to his belt. "This will be a lot less tiresome than having to wear it around your neck all day," she told him. "It's on the automatic setting, so use it just as it is, okay?"

"Okay," Davy responded, giving her a hug. "I promise to take really good care of it and we'll have lots of photos to show you when we get back."

"Let's get going, Davy," Anna urged him. "Mary's getting impatient." The boy laughed and the two, waving enthusiastically to Mom and Jim, left by the kitchen door with a jovial, though invisible to all but Davy, Racer bounding ahead of them.

"This way, children," he called over his shoulder. "Follow me!"

Mom and Jim stepped outside and watched their retreating figures until they were mere dots meandering across the meadow. When Davy and Anna slipped entirely from view, they turned and headed, hand-in-hand, toward the now strangely quiet house. "This is quite a milestone for you today, Kate," Jim observed, giving her hand a loving squeeze. "I know letting them go off on their own, even with Racer with them, wasn't easy for you to do."

"It wasn't," she admitted, smiling up at him, "and neither will my trying not to worry, but I'm determined to do better in my faith walk."

"That's my girl," Jim said encouragingly as he opened the door for her. "Remember, it doesn't have to be any bigger than a mustard seed to accomplish great things."

Chapter 4

A Picnic and a Peril

The three explorers traversed the meadow, Racer in the lead, with Davy and Anna bringing up the rear. Anna was enchanted by the myriad of colorful wildflowers peppered here and there amidst the tall grass. "Look at all these beautiful flowers!" she exclaimed. "Let's pick some for Mom on our way back."

"Good idea," Davy agreed. "Move a bit to the right, Anna. Racer's changing direction." Davy knew it would have made more sense for his sister to follow him so she'd know exactly where to go, but because she was hesitant about being in the back of the line, he offered to be the rudder on this expedition. Realistically, he knew Racer was their true guide, and all he had to do was verbalize the squirrel's moves to Anna.

"It's not too much farther until we're at the trailhead," Racer called to him. "Let's see if you can see the sign before I point it out to you, okay, Davy?"

"Okay," he shouted.

"Okay to what?" Anna wished to know.

"Racer wants to see if we can spot the sign for the trail before he shows it to us."

"Oooh!" Anna said enthusiastically. "I hope I see it first!"

"Just keep your eyes open and maybe you will," Davy told her. It wasn't a minute later when Davy's sharp eyes spied the sign. Anna gave no indication that she had spotted it at all. He wanted his sister to think she was the first to see it, so he decided to do some prompting. "Do you see it yet, Anna?"

She shaded her eyes. "No, not yet."

"Look a little harder," he urged her.

Anna stopped walking for a moment so she could better scan the woods, which were looming ahead. "Yes!" she squealed and pointed. "There it is! I see it!"

"Good work, little one," Racer praised her. "Now, all you two have to do is head in that direction and we'll be well on our way."

"Racer says you did good work, Anna," Davy told her.

"Thanks, Racer!" she sang out, and began to skip through to tall grasses to reach the sign as quickly as she could.

"Slow down," Davy admonished as he trotted behind her. "You might make Mary fall out of her sling." Anna slowed down immediately at that thought, and both proceeded to the trailhead at a much more sedate pace. When they arrived, Racer was perched on top of the sign, sporting his lopsided grin.

"So far, so good," he said. "Now, let's all have a drink of water before we start down the trail."

"It's time for some water, Anna," Davy said. The children unhooked their bottles from their belts and took several refreshing swigs. Davy then held his bottle to Racer's lips so the squirrel could quench his thirst.

"Davy," Anna scolded when she saw him tip his bottle, "you shouldn't waste your water like that."

"I'm not," he said. "I'm giving some to Racer."

"Oh," she backtracked. "I guess, because I can't see him, I forgot for a moment he was here with us."

"Forget me?" Racer proclaimed with feigned indignation, spluttering water droplets everywhere. "How could anyone forget such a stunning creature as I?" Davy laughed at the squirrel's dramatic outburst, and Anna was amazed by the miniature shower falling from a seemingly clear sky. When it dawned on her that Racer, himself, was the cause of the sprinkles, she moved closer to the signpost.

"I'm sorry, Racer," she apologized. "I can't see you, but because of the water, I know where you are. That makes me happy."

"Believing in something you can't see is easier than you might think, my children," Racer told them. Davy dutifully repeated the words to his sister. "Are we ready to push on?"

"Time to head up the trail, Anna," Davy announced. They refastened their water bottles and embarked on the next leg of their journey. The coolness of the forest, in contrast to the warmth of the meadow, was pleasingly refreshing. As they sauntered along, they stopped intermittently to admire a tiny flower, or a rotting log with an especially abundant growth of fungi and mosses, or the occasional songbird they spotted. Davy snapped as many pictures as he could. After taking a multitude of photos with Anna in front of this tree or standing in the middle of the trail, he thought it high time that she take some photos of him.

"Here, Anna," he said, offering her the camera. "Take some shots of me beside this large boulder. It's impressive!" After reminding his sister how to hold the camera and which button to push, she clicked away and, to his delight, took several decent shots. His shiner, almost imperceptible now, fortunately did not look like anything but a natural shadow. Davy was grateful for this, as he felt they were making great memories to share with Mom and Jim, and that was all that mattered.

"Davy," said Racer, bounding back to them from where he had been scouting the trail ahead, "give me the camera and let me take a picture of the two of you together."

"You know how to use this?" Davy asked incredulously.

"But of course," the squirrel reassured him. "Bob has a camera just like it, and I've watched him use it multiple times."

"It won't be too heavy for you to hold?" the boy asked anxiously, knowing how upset Mom would be if the camera was damaged.

"Not for the few moments it takes to snap it," Racer told him. "Go stand by that boulder again with Anna. There, that's it. Smile, you two!"

For Anna, that was no problem, as seeing her mother's camera suspended in mid-air made her giggle uncontrollably. There was a successful click, and then Racer, regrettably, lowered the camera as gently as he could. "It's just a bit too heavy after all," he admitted sorrowfully. "I would have liked to take more."

"Maybe you can," Davy said brightly.

"How is that?"

"Let's look for a place to set both you and the camera while we stand in front of it. Then all you have to do is push the button."

"Splendid idea, my child!" Racer declared happily. "We'll do just that. Perhaps we'll have a better opportunity for picture-taking when we're picnicking at the creek. There are lots of large rocks that we could place the camera, and yours truly, on."

"Awesome," said Davy, picking up the camera gingerly and easing it into its case.

"How far is it to the creek, Racer?" Anna asked.

"Not more than half a mile by my estimation," he answered.

Davy, thinking this distance might sound too intimidating to his sister, merely said, "We'll be there shortly."

"Good, because Mary is already getting hungry and so am I."

"Make that three of us," Racer piped up.

With that, the three strode off again, this time with fewer stops and at a more determined pace. Davy was eagerly looking forward to sitting by Big Bear Creek with its ceaseless and soothing chatter as it flowed over and around the stones lining its bed.

It would be even cooler there, as he knew from his experience last Saturday when he met with Racer at another part of it. Although his legs weren't particularly tired, Davy's stomach was beginning to growl and rumble irritatingly. He was greatly relieved when he heard, faintly at first, but waxing louder with every step he took, the sound of the tumbling water.

"It won't be much longer, Anna," he told her. "How are you holding up?"

"I'm fine," she said, none too convincingly.

"You'll be even better after we eat and rest by the creek for a while," he said cheerfully. "Just make sure Mary doesn't get near the water."

Anna halted in the middle of the trail and whirled around to face him. "Davy, how could you say such a thing?" she chided him. "Don't you think I know how to look after my friend?"

"I'm sorry, Anna," Davy replied with alacrity, regretting that his sister had mistaken his casual teasing for an insult. He definitely, especially without Mom around, did not want to make her cry. "I was only kidding, really. I know you'll be extra careful with her."

"It's okay, I guess," she said slowly and with just the slightest hint of sadness in her voice. "I thought for a minute that you didn't trust me."

Davy strode the few steps it took to catch up with her, and then walked beside her as they continued to their destination. The path conveniently broadened to accommodate two traveling side by side. "You know what, Anna?" he told her. "I used to not trust you, that is, before we arrived here at the farm, but now I do. I mean that; honest, cross my heart, hope to die mean it."

His sister bit her lower lip and, for one precarious moment, Davy feared the very tears he had hoped to quell were on the brink of descending. Anna took a deep breath and, to his immeasurable relief, greeted him with a smile. "I'm glad you trust me," she said. "I trust you, too."

Davy returned her smile and pulled ever so slightly on her long braid. "I know," he assured her. And at that very moment, in the deepest recesses of his heart, he knew that she always had.

***

"I'm here at the creek, Davy," Racer hollered in the loudest voice he could muster. "One more bend in the trail, and you'll be here, too!"

Throwing caution to the wind in his excitement, Davy exhorted Anna to run along with him for the remainder of the trail. She didn't have to be asked twice. Their feet flew as if they had sprouted wings, nimbly dodging tree roots and the occasional large rock along the path, as they sprinted toward an imaginary finish line. When they came around the last turn, there, just as Racer had promised, was Big Bear Creek, sparkling and gurgling as it made its way to the lake. Racer, Davy saw, was perched atop a broad, somewhat flat, moss-cushioned boulder. "I think this will do for a picnic table, don't you, Davy?" he asked.

The boy nodded in agreement. "Let's eat our lunches on that large rock, Anna," he suggested. "We'll have a great view of the creek from there."

"Sounds good to me," she said.

They scrambled onto the top of the accommodating rock. Davy removed Mary from her sling for Anna and retrieved their lunches from his backpack. Any onlookers would have been mystified as to why, when only two people were sitting there, the spread was being laid out for three. They would have been further confounded as they witnessed sandwiches, pickles, grapes, and deviled eggs floating weightlessly in midair and vanishing one bite at a time. At first, Anna was giggling so hard at the sight that she could barely eat her own lunch. Fortunately, her appetite finally got the better of her and she dug in with relish, sharing everything, of course, with Mary, whom she had placed in her lap.

Davy eyed the squirrel curiously. "Racer, I know you ate under the table when you were on our last picnic and at our house, but there was one time you were in plain sight. Why didn't anyone see the blueberries hovering in the air?"

The squirrel popped the last bite of his ham sandwich into his mouth and reached for the turkey one. "It took extra effort on my part," he explained. "The energy it takes is not nearly as draining as it is when I make myself visible to others, but it can be tiresome after a while. Since it's only the three of us and we're tucked away in the wilderness, I can simply relax and enjoy this sumptuous meal. Another pickle, please?"

"Davy, I was wondering," said Anna, "will any of the other Old Ones join us today?"

"They could," Racer mumbled through his pickle. "We are ever roaming these woods, checking in on the mortal creatures of our kind. Mrs. Racer would have come today, but she had to visit a squirrel family living east of The Glade. A young one hurt her paw and Mrs. Racer was going to doctor it for her." After Davy had passed on his friend's comments to Anna, she quietly continued to eat, but seemed preoccupied. Racer noticed this change in her demeanor and suggested to Davy that he ask her what was on her mind. The boy complied.

"I was just wondering," she said, "because I heard Mom say Racer was like a guardian angel for us, is that what the Old Ones are to all the creatures in this place?"

"I suppose you could call us that," Racer observed. "We certainly do our best to protect and aid our counterparts whenever and wherever we can. Are there any pickles left? No? Could you pass me a devilled egg, then?"

Davy relayed Racer's answer and gave the squirrel the last of the eggs. The three of them continued to eat for a while without exchanging any words. Instead, they listened to the creek's constant, yet soothing, voice and admired all the greenery of the forest. Full and content at last, Davy stuffed his trash into the backpack, took out the camera, and snapped some pictures of Big Bear Creek and its idyllic surroundings. He then remembered he wanted to get some photos of both Anna and himself, and began scanning the area for a suitable place to set the camera so it would be easy for Racer to use it.

"What are you looking for, Davy?" Anna asked as she picked up after herself.

"A place to put this camera so Racer can take our picture," he said.

"Why not on this rock we're sitting on?" Racer asked as he brushed crumbs from his whiskers. "You could stand right over there by those rhododendrons, and I could snap some from here."

"Awesome! C'mon, Anna. Stand over here with me," Davy said. He set the camera on the boulder and aimed it in the direction Racer had indicated. Both children slipped off the rock and arranged themselves in front of the deep-green, leafy bushes. The squirrel squinted through the viewfinder.

"Move a little to the left," he instructed. "Stand closer together. That's it! Stay right there and say, 'pickle.'"

"Pickle!" they shouted for the first of five more successful shots.

"There, that should do it," Racer declared. "Now, my children, I am quite full and somewhat drowsy, so I think I'll take a little snooze. Why don't you take off your shoes and socks and wade in the creek for a while?"

"That sounds like fun," Davy said. "Anna, Racer's going to take a nap, so why don't we wade in the creek?"

"It's awfully cold," she warned him, recalling her recent encounter with the lake.

"Aw, c'mon," he cajoled, "you don't have to stay in long if you don't want to."

"Oh, all right," Anna conceded, somewhat reluctantly.

By the time they had their shoes and socks off, rolled up their jeans, and were negotiating their way on tender feet toward the stream, Racer was already snoring resoundingly. "I don't know how he does that," Davy said.

"Does what?" Anna asked.

"Fall asleep so quickly. He's already snoring."

"I wish I could hear it," she said. "I bet it sounds funny."

"It's kind of like Jim's when he falls asleep in his chair and his mouth opens." Anna laughed at this comparison, as she could easily hear Jim's snuffling and snorting in her mind.

Davy was the first to ease his foot into the water, but jerked back involuntarily. Anna had been right; it was icy! Determined not to let it get the best of him, he gritted his teeth and forced himself to plunge it in all at once as he always did to his whole body when, completely dry, he'd leap off the side of the pool and into the water. He felt a shock of cold run through his foot, but he brought his other one in right behind it. Anna was sitting on the creek bank merely brushing her toes across the surface. "How can you do that?" she asked when she saw Davy standing ankle-deep in the rushing water."

"You were right. It is cold," he admitted, "but, little by little, I'm getting used to it."

When he trusted his footing better, Davy waded farther out into the stream. The rocks were smooth and worn, and felt a bit slick, so he moved slowly and meticulously. Anna, never one to be bested by her brother, screwed up her courage and slid her feet entirely into the creek. She squealed so loudly, Davy thought she might have hurt herself and turned to see. "It's so cold, so cold, so cold!" Anna shrieked with laughter. "It's much colder than the lake was!"

"It won't feel so bad in a minute," Davy assured her. "Just be careful, because it's kind of slippery."

"Good thing I left Mary on the boulder," she said as her feet sensed what Davy had cautioned her about. "It's one thing if I fall in and get wet, but not her, not ever again!'

"You don't want to fall either, Anna," he warned her. "Walking home in wet jeans would be pretty miserable."

"How would you know?"

"I just do," he said. Davy remembered how heavy and cumbersome his jeans in the washing machine had felt that day when he was desperately trying to find the key to Grandpa's box. Then it struck him like a bolt of lightning. He had been so immersed in the drama of the last two days since The Naming, the ceremony required of him before he could read Grandpa Will's stories, he had neglected to look at them or even tell his family of his wondrous find. Davy was so tempted to tell Anna about them right then and there, but thought it best to ask Racer first. Now that everyone knew of the Old Ones' existence, he didn't think there would be a problem in sharing the stories. He vowed to ask Racer at the first opportunity.

The children waded for about ten more minutes before deciding, after Davy had almost lost his footing because his feet were going numb, it was time to get out of the water. "How are we going to dry off?" Anna wondered aloud.

"Didn't Mom hand us extra napkins today?" Davy asked.

"Oh, that's right, she did," Anna recalled.

Once their feet were sufficiently dry, Davy and Anna put their socks and shoes back on and, in an attempt to get warm, stretched their legs out in a patch of sunlight that filtered through the leaves. Racer was still dozing, though he wasn't snoring as loudly now. Quietly, so as to not disturb his friend, Davy reclaimed the camera, placed it back in its case, and hooked it onto his belt. Anna had insisted on keeping her sling on, because she was sure they could never figure out how Mom had fastened it, and Mary was snugly inside it once again.

"It looks like you're ready to head home," Davy observed.

"Yes, I think I am, and I know Mary is ready," Anna replied. "Do you need to wake Racer up, or is he up already?"

"I'll wake him," he said, standing up, stretching, and heading back to the boulder where the squirrel reclined so peacefully. Davy was just reaching out to gently shake him when Racer sat bolt upright, any lingering drowsiness in his eyes replaced by an intense look of alarm. The boy jumped back in surprise. Not wanting to frighten Anna, Davy hissed softly, but urgently, "Racer, what is it? What's wrong?"

"Gunshots!" he cried. "Gather your things quickly, child. I must get you back home as fast as I can."

"Gunshots?" Davy whispered hoarsely as he hastily zipped up his pack and hoisted it onto his shoulders. "I didn't hear anything. Are you sure you weren't dreaming?"

"Davy, you forget that my hearing is exceptionally keen," he said. "Don't say anything to Anna. We don't want to scare her. Just tell her it is past time to head for home, and you need to move as quickly as your legs will safely carry you." With that said, Racer leaped up the trunk of the nearest tree and into its branches. "I will keep an eye on you both from above while seeing if I can spy the source of what I know I heard," he hollered down to Davy. "Tell Anna it's time to go!"

When Davy returned to his sister, she instantly saw the worried look on his face. "What's wrong, Davy? Did Racer leave us?"

"No, but he says we need to hurry home because we've stayed later than we should have," he told her. "I need you to walk just as fast as you can. I'll be right behind you, okay?"

"Okay," Anna said, but Davy detected the hint of tears in her eyes. Though he'd tried valiantly to conceal it, she had read his fear.

Mustering up his courage, Davy managed to give his sister a reassuring smile, a salute, and a "Move out, troops" command which she readily obeyed. He had to admit that he had never seen Anna walk as briskly as she did now, and he was relieved she hadn't balked at his request. As they hurried along, Davy strained to hear even the faintest report of gunfire, but was met only by the majestic stillness of the woods and ever-fading murmur of Big Bear Creek. Every five minutes or so, Racer would call out words of encouragement to help both children maintain their progress.

"You're both doing great, my child," said the squirrel. "Tell Anna I'm proud of her so she'll keep going strong."

"Anna," Davy said, "Racer wants you to know he's proud of you for being such a strong hiker. Let's show him how we can keep up the pace."

"All right," Anna said a bit breathlessly, but the support of the squirrel she could neither see nor hear revived her resolve, and she forged ahead even faster than before.

When at last they reached the signpost and saw the meadow sprawling invitingly before them, Davy caught the faintest echo of gunshots, still distant, yet insistent and repeated as if more than one person were shooting. It was at this point that Racer leaped to the ground and hopped up on his shoulder. "I believe whoever is firing those guns has made it to the ridge and is possibly near The Glade," he told Davy. "That is far enough away from here that you won't be in any peril crossing the meadow."

"Are you sure?" Davy asked, his voice hushed, as both children tried to catch their breaths before leaving the soothing shade for the shimmering heat of the open field.

"Positive, my child," Racer said. "I would never send you into harm's way. You know that."

"Yes, I know, Racer, but what about you? Where are you going now?"

"Back to The Glade," he declared. "But don't you fret. I'm arriving there in high-speed mode, so there will be no way a stray bullet can hit me."

"A stray bullet?" Davy blanched with dread at the thought that his dearest friend could be hurt in any way.

"All will be well with me, so don't you worry," he said, patting Davy's head affectionately and planting a farewell kiss on his cheek. "I think it's all right, too, for you both to pick a lovely bouquet for your mother as you originally planned. How happy that will make her!" Then Racer, much to Davy's surprise, leapt onto Anna's shoulder and gave her a quick kiss, too. Jumping down, the squirrel disappeared in a twinkling.

"What was that?" Anna asked, rubbing her cheek where Racer had tickled it.

"That was Racer giving you a kiss good-bye," Davy informed her.

"Really? Then, he's leaving us?"

"Just for now," he said, patting her head as Racer had done his. "He'll be back as soon as he can, and we know the way this time."

"You're right," Anna said. "If I squint really hard, I can almost see the house from here."

"Then let's head for it and, Anna," he smiled and his sister registered the look of relief on her brother's face, "Racer told me not to forget to pick flowers for Mom along the way."

Chapter 5

The Fairchilds to the Rescue

"Come, Maggie," Kate called to the old dog cheerily as she held the kitchen door with one arm and a wicker basket with the other. "Let's go out and fetch the clothes off the line." Maggie staggered to her feet, her fluffy tail waving agreeably, and accepted Kate's invitation.

"Going outside again, Kate?" Jim remarked from his seat at the kitchen table, looking up at her over his reading glasses. He had been perusing the same wildlife book which had held Davy's attention had only days before.

"I want to see if the clothes are dry," she insisted.

"And thirty minutes ago, it was to pull some weeds in the garden, and twenty minutes before that, it was to bird watch, and...."

"Okay, okay," she laughed and blushed. "I guess my mustard seed needs a little more water and sunlight."

Jim laid the book and his glasses on the table and strode over to her where she stood, hesitatingly, in the doorway. He gently removed the basket from her grasp and gave her a kiss. "You've actually done better than I thought you would," he said with a smile. "You'll get used to it as the summer rolls along and, as for the clothes, let me help you get those in."

"Thank you, honey," she said gratefully as she leaned into his shoulder. "I would truly love your help."

"You've got it," he assured her as they strolled outside together.

Maggie had finished her business and was patiently waiting for them by the clothesline. After seeing the basket, she had known exactly where they were headed. "What a good dog you are, Maggie," Kate praised her, bending down to give her head several loving strokes. "Are you missing Davy and Anna?"

"Woof, woof!" Maggie barked affirmatively.

"Jim," Kate stated, "I do believe this dog understands almost everything we say to her."

"She's remarkable, at that," he agreed, reaching up to remove several items from the line and depositing them in the basket. "Grandpa always claimed she was the smartest dog he ever owned, and I believe it."

"Is it any wonder?" Kate interjected. "After all, it was Maggie who saw the cell phone that Ronnie was taking the photos with, and was able to fit the pieces together. If it weren't for her, Racer and the others...." Her voice trailed off as her own words transported her back into a world to which she had only been introduced yesterday, but that now seemed to be a part of her life that had somehow existed within her all along.

While Jim continued removing clothes from the line, Kate stood as if she were entranced. When he dropped them into the basket, he glanced at his wife's face. She was gazing at nothing in particular, standing stock-still as if locked in a faraway dream. He approached her and placed his arms around her waist. "Come back to me, Kate," he whispered, "I miss you."

She shuddered ever so slightly, blinked her eyes, and turned to face Jim. He could tell by her expression and focus that she had returned to the present. "Where was I?" she inquired, still feeling slightly disoriented by her experience.

"Lost in Davy's world," Jim responded matter-of-factly.

"In Davy's world? How can that be?" Kate longed to know what her husband meant by this remark.

"You need to remember that I lived here with Grandpa and Grandma for many years. Not to alarm you, but the expression you had on your face just now was identical to the one I saw on Grandpa's face countless times. I never actually understood what it was all about until yesterday." Jim took Kate gently, but firmly, by the shoulders, searched her face, and stared deeply into her eyes. "I think," he said slowly and deliberately, "you are the reason why Davy has The Gift."

"You don't mean I have it, too, do you?" Kate stammered in disbelief.

"Yes, I do," he said, "but it's been dormant for many, many years. What took place at The Glade began to awaken that part of you which was sleeping so soundly inside."

Kate was momentarily at a loss for words. Her world, reliable and practical, had suddenly spiraled into the unknown, replacing the woman she thought she was with one she didn't recognize at all. She looked at Jim pleadingly, and asked, "What should I do now?"

"I don't think 'doing' is your answer," he replied. "I think it's 'being.' Just go with the flow and be open to the moment."

"In other words, don't force the feelings, but simply allow them to develop if that's what they choose to do?"

"Exactly," Jim confirmed.

"That's easier said than done," Kate said softly, hanging her head.

Jim pulled her to him and held her close. "That's because you are such a doer, Kate, always taking care of the family, planning ahead in everything, working so hard at your job. It's time for a rest, don't you think? And, what was that you said just the other day about this place making you feel like a kid again? It seems to have the same effect on everyone to a greater or lesser degree, because I feel it, too. In your case, however, it may be to a greater degree in every way."

Neither spoke for several moments. Kate listened to the calming beat of Jim's heart as she rested her head on his chest, and allowed his words to penetrate from mind to heart. She once again felt calm and at peace with herself, no matter what self that might now be. "Thank you, Jim," she whispered at last.

"You're welcome," he responded, and then added, "If you look toward the meadow, Kate, I know you will see what you've been waiting for."

Kate immediately raised her head; expectations high, she intently scrutinized the meadow. "Yes! There they are," she exclaimed, pointing at Davy and Anna with utmost delight, relief, and joy.

"Yep, here come our two explorers, looking, from what I can tell, none the worse for wear," Jim observed, also happy to see Davy and Anna returning all in one piece.

Maggie, even at that great distance, caught a whiff of the children's scent on the breeze, and began barking enthusiastically, her tail wagging a mile a minute. When they heard Maggie's welcome, Davy and Anna looked up to see Mom and Jim standing in the yard and began waving vigorously at them. Anna's glorious bouquet swayed and bobbed crazily above her head as she heralded her approach.

"Looks like they've brought you a present, Kate," Jim acknowledged with a satisfied grin.

"Oh, yes, it does!" Kate beamed. "How incredibly thoughtful of them!"

When the children emerged from the meadow and onto the lawn, Maggie got up and trotted out to meet them. Anna welcomed her with a few pats on the head and then kept on going while Davy knelt down to give his dog a tremendous hug. He was rewarded with a liberal face washing of the slobbery kind. "Let's go, Maggie," he told her when he stood up at last. "I want to show Mom and Jim the pictures we took."

"Woof!" Maggie acknowledged, and off they went. When they arrived at where Mom and Jim were standing, Anna had already exchanged hugs and was bending their ears with all the details of their morning. They continued to listen as they both offered hugs to Davy.

"Big Bear Creek was so cold to wade in, much colder than the lake, Mom, but we did it anyway while Racer was taking a nap. You know, Jim, Davy said Racer snores like you do when you fall asleep in your chair at home. And when we ate our lunch, it was so funny to see sandwiches and pickles dancing in the air. I could hardly stop laughing long enough to eat my own!"

"And," Davy managed to interrupt when Anna paused for a much-needed breath, "we took lots of photos. Racer even took some of Anna and me together because we thought you'd like them."

"I can't wait to see them," Mom declared, hugging her children yet again.

"Why don't you go on into the house with the kids, Kate," Jim suggested. "I'll bet they could use some lemonade right about now. I'll get the rest of the clothes for you."

Mom laughed. "Not that I've been any help at all out here," she said, "but I'm so glad you'll finish the chore. C'mon, kids!"

"I'll be right there, Mom!" Davy called as Anna and she headed for the kitchen door.

Once the ladies were safely inside, Jim said, "Okay, Davy, you have something to tell that only I need to hear, am I right?"

"Yes, sir," he said as Jim continued to remove clothes from the line.

"Let's have it, then."

Davy cleared his throat as if doing so would make the news easier to tell. "When we were just getting ready to leave the creek, Racer woke up all upset, saying he heard gunshots."

"Gunshots? Where?" Jim asked, genuinely disturbed by this information.

"He wasn't exactly sure and I didn't hear anything, at least not at first," said Davy. "Racer stayed with us on the trail to the meadow, but up in the trees to see if he could better tell where they were coming from. We didn't let Anna know about them, but I got her to hurry as fast as she could because she thought we were late. When we got to the meadow, Racer told me we were safe as he felt sure the shots were coming from the other side of the ridge toward The Glade. That's when I heard them."

"Grandpa never allowed hunting on this property," Jim noted grimly. "It's still not allowed, and this isn't even hunting season. And you said Racer heard many shots?"

"That's what he told me," Davy said. "I did, too, once I could hear them."

"That certainly doesn't sound like hunting," Jim said with a scowl. "It's more like random shooting just to hear your own gun firing off. I don't like the sound of this one bit."

"Are you going to call Sheriff Peabody?" Davy asked.

"I'll see him at church on Sunday, so I'll just talk to him then," Jim said, removing the last item of clothing from the line. "By that time, maybe Racer will have something more definite to tell us."

"I sure hope so," Davy said wistfully, "and I sure hope he wasn't hurt trying to get back to The Glade."

"Racer can be hurt by a bullet?" Jim asked, incredulous.

"By what he said and how he said it, I think he could be," said Davy.

"Well, let's just pray he's safe and sound, shall we?" Jim said with a sigh, patting Davy's shoulder comfortingly before bending over to pick up the loaded laundry basket. In that fraction of a second, Jim's fickle back decided this was the perfect time to go out on him. He let fly an agonizing shout which frightened Davy out of his wits, and dropped to his knees, his face contorted from the excruciating pain. "Davy," he gasped, "my back. Get your mother."

The boy flew into the house. "Mom! Mom! Come quick!" he yelled frantically. "Jim's hurt his back!"

Kate, with Anna at her heels, dashed out of the house and was by Jim's side in seconds flat. "Oh, Jim, you poor thing!" Kate moaned sympathetically.

"I can't get up," he grunted, "not without help."

"Davy!" Mom ordered briskly. "Go inside and dial Mr. and Mrs. Fairchild; their number is right beside the phone. Ask them to both come if they can. I'm not strong enough to help Jim by myself. Go! Hurry!"

Once again, Davy found himself racing for the house and making tracks to the telephone. He was grateful Jim had demonstrated how to use the old-fashioned instrument, or he would have been at a total loss as to what to do at this point. The dial felt awkward to his small fingers, but he managed, in what seemed like forever, to place the call.

"Hello?" Mrs. Fairchild's pleasant voice answered.

"Hi, Mrs. Fairchild, it's Davy. We need you and Mr. Fairchild to come over quick!"

"What is it, darling?" she asked anxiously, hearing the urgency in his plea.

"It's Jim," Davy told her. "He's thrown out his back and Mom can't help him up."

"Not to worry," she assured him. "Go tell your mother we'll be there in a snap."

They hung up without even saying good-bye, and Davy sped back out to the yard where Jim crouched like a wounded animal. "They're on their way!" he shouted.

"Thank the Lord!" Mom exclaimed. "Hang in there, honey, help is coming."

"This makes no sense," Jim groaned. "I carry Anna down the trail, I spend all morning hoeing the garden, and nothing happens. I go to lift a doggone laundry basket, and *wham*, out it goes. Ouch!" Jim winced as a fresh spasm of pain seared through him.

Kate stroked his hair soothingly and kissed his forehead. "It just might be those very things you did which led up to this," she said comfortingly.

Davy stood next to Anna who clutched Mary hard to her chest, her eyes filling with tears. "Don't cry," he whispered to her. "Jim's going to be all right."

"I know. I just don't like seeing him hurt," she whispered back. "It scares me."

"It scares me, too," Davy admitted, thinking his stepdad, always so strong and self-reliant, must absolutely detest being reduced to this state of helplessness. He so hoped the Fairchilds would arrive soon. Within that very minute, Davy's wish was granted as their truck, heard long before it was seen, hurtled around the bend. Davy thought Mr. Fairchild must be driving even faster than he had the other day when he had ridden with Maggie in the truck bed, and he wondered what Mrs. Fairchild thought of this reckless speed. The truck screeched to a halt and the Fairchilds, bounding from it, rushed over to Mom and Jim.

Mrs. Fairchild began giving orders, something at which, Davy had gleaned from their first evening together, she was extremely adept. "Kate, go inside and roll that leather office chair into the kitchen near a plug outlet. Davy, take this heating pad and plug it in. Anna, you stand and hold the door open for Bob and Jim. Bob, I can help you get him up, but after that I think it would be best if he tried to get somewhat comfortable leaning on you. Of course, I'll walk alongside in case my support is needed."

Everyone hastened to follow Susie's directions, leaving the Fairchilds with the difficult task of getting Jim to his feet without causing him another round of stabbing pain. Bob knelt on one side of him with Susie on the other. Jim lifted his arm to Bob's shoulder. Bob grabbed his hand firmly to hold Jim in place should another wave of agonizing pain hit his back. This accomplished, Jim placed his other arm around Susie's shoulder and she did the same. He was surprised by her firm, yet gentle, grip. "Now comes the hard part, Jim," she warned. "You're going to have to work with us no matter how badly it hurts."

"I know," he told her. "Unfortunately, I've been here before."

"All right, then," she said. "Roll onto the balls of your feet and, on the count of three, Bob and I are going to stand up and, good Lord willing, you'll come with us. Ready? One, two, three!"

Davy was abundantly thankful he wasn't watching Jim's attempt to stand as the cry of anguish he emitted at that moment would break the hardest of hearts. Mom, who had just positioned the chair as Susie had instructed, clutched its arm hard, her face stricken with grief. Anna, who had the misfortune of witnessing it all, was crying unabashedly. Seeing this, Davy scooted to the door to relieve her of her unfortunate duty so she could retreat to the living room where Jim wouldn't have to see her tears. He had enough to deal with as it was. Moving slowly, but deliberately, Bob supported Jim unwaveringly as he hobbled, little by little, across the lawn and up the stairs. Once inside, Susie picked up the heating pad and motioned to Bob to guide Jim toward the chair. "Before you sit down, Jim, dear," she said, "I need you to show me the exact location of your pain so I can fasten the heating pad in a way that will most benefit you."

Weakly, Jim laid his left hand on the lower left part of his back. "Good," she said, and promptly fell to work, attaching the heating pad, which, she declared, was warming up nicely. "Kate, hold the chair firmly and we'll ease Jim into it as carefully as we can."

They successfully lowered Jim into the seat and helped him to position his back where it had support and would aggravate him the least. The process was not without several more jabs of pain, but none as severe as when he had initially stood up. Jim leaned his head back and closed his eyes. "Thanks so much," he mumbled.

"Don't mention it," said Bob. We're just happy to be of assistance."

"This heating pad should help tremendously," said Susie, "but I left some things in the truck that should help as well. Kate, dear, could you pour a glass of water for Jim, please?" Susie exited the kitchen door and returned momentarily with two small bottles of pills. "This one is for the pain, and the other will help Jim's back muscles relax so he can rest," she explained to Kate, and made sure she understood the proper dosage.

"How did you happen to have these?" Kate wondered.

Susie replied, "My back went out last fall when I stressed it while planting hundreds of bulbs in Mr. Will's yard and ours. It turned out I didn't need to take many before I felt better, but I saved them just in case something happened again."

"They're certainly a Godsend now," Kate declared. "Thank you so much, Susie, for all Bob and you have done today."

"No thanks necessary," Susie assured her. "Now, let's get the first dose of these into that husband of yours so he can start feeling better."

Kate handed the pills and the glass of water to Jim who took them gratefully. "Can you believe I left my back pain medicine in Atlanta?" he said regretfully. "Susie, you're a lifesaver."

"This should get you through, Jim," she said. "And if not, you can visit Dr. Jacobs over in Bryson City. He's a fine man, not to mention a fine doctor."

"Let's hope it doesn't come to that." Jim smiled, feeling better already from the heating pad's toasty warmth.

At that moment, Anna emerged from the living room, her face red and splotchy from weeping. She looked so pathetic, Davy desperately tried to conjure up something that would cheer her and allow her 'water to go the right way' as Racer so creatively put it. Even Mary, hanging limply from his sister's hand, looked as though she, too, could use some encouragement. *That's it! The bear! I haven't given Smokey to her yet. He's still hidden on the porch!*

"C'mon, Anna," he whispered to her, "I have something to give you."

"Give me?" she asked, still sniffling.

"Yep, it's out on the porch," he said with a smile. "With all that's been going on these past couple of days, I forgot all about it." Anna dutifully followed her brother to the porch and closed her eyes at his request in order to be properly surprised. Davy fetched Smokey from where he had hidden him behind a photo of their father, concealed the bear behind his back, and returned to face his sister. "Before I show you your gift," he told her, "I want you to know I think Mary will like it, too."

"Oh, please, please," she begged, "can we look now?"

Davy held Smokey in front of him and said, "Open your eyes."

Anna did and her face transformed instantly from its melancholy gloom into the veritable image of sheer delight. "It's Smokey!" she exclaimed gleefully. "Look, Mary, he's just like the Smokey in our coloring book!" Anna joyfully removed the toy bear from her brother's hands and gathered it, along with Mary, into a welcoming embrace. "We're all going to be the best of friends," she declared and, with a most appreciative gesture to Davy, added, "you are the best brother in the whole world!"

"Thank Jim, too," he told her, feeling humbled by her generous praise. "I found Smokey, but he was the one who bought him."

"Oh, I will," she said. "I'll do that right now!" Anna skipped off to the kitchen, returned to the carefree spirit she was ever meant to be.

Davy ploddingly followed. He was glad to see his sister's happiness restored, but his qualms about Racer suddenly reared their ugly heads. *Why does Racer have to worry about bullets? What if one, even when he is in high speed, hits him? Does he become visible so the shooter can finish him off?* Davy shuddered at this last thought and tried his best to wipe his mind clean of misgivings. He knew he must wait patiently for his questions to find their answers, and prayed that Racer would return soon to put to rest all his fears.

Chapter 6

The Silver Bullet

After Sheriff Peabody departed, Ronnie sat staring at his cell phone. Feelings of anger and despair welled up within him. All the plans he had so carefully and, he thought, brilliantly orchestrated had been shattered by the incriminating evidence he had neglected to delete from his cell phone. Now he was not only out of the land which he had been determined to develop, but he had also spent thousands of dollars in bribes that he would never recover. The very thought of this made him nauseous, and caused his bandaged hand to throb even more than it already had been. Miserably, but just to make sure the sheriff wasn't bluffing, Ronnie forced himself to check his phone for the photos. When he saw them exactly as he remembered, he was overcome by a fresh wave of ire. In his fit of fury, Ronnie threw his phone down on the sofa, reached for his empty tea glass, and hurled it with all his might at the fireplace.

The sound of shattering glass brought Betty Rae running from the kitchen. "What was that?" she asked in alarm.

"Get out of here, woman!" Ronnie roared.

She took one look at his face, infused with rage, and beat a hasty retreat. Ronnie proceeded to pace the floor like a caged lion, directing every curse word he could conjure up at Jim. Even though Peabody hadn't said anything outright, Ronnie was convinced his rotten cousin had everything to do with this sour turn of events. "That greedy, no-good, sonuva...he growled. "He gets all that land and won't even sell me a square inch. I deserved to have some of that property when Will died. Jim wasn't even around to look after the ungrateful old man who left me nothing when I did so much for him. I bet, yes, I just *bet* Jim was the one who convinced the old geezer not to leave me a thing. One way or another, I'm going to make him pay, and pay good!"

As Ronnie continued striding and spewing, his initial anger began to subside, and his thoughts became more clear and rational. He realized that what he needed to do was mull over every detail of the situation and come up with a plan. The question of how his cell phone even came into Sheriff Peabody's custody, and how the man knew to look for the photos, pressed heavily upon him. Bill Cunningham, his foreman, had sworn he had seen Ronnie arrive at work that day with the phone on his belt, yet it mysteriously went missing from the desk drawer he always placed it in. Had one of the workers sneaked in and stolen it? Ronnie quickly dismissed this idea, as no one but Bill had even come near the trailer all morning.

Then there were the invisible forces that had attacked and so terrified the entire crew, they fled from the work site. Even Buddy and Sammy had been scared witless by an unseen power which had thrown them to the ground up on the trail. And how, if they swore they took their rifles with them, had the guns come to be neatly stacked against the trailer? Was that mountain, as his workers claimed, haunted? Ronnie didn't believe in ghosts and refused to accept this supposition as the answer. But if not that, what else could it have possibly been?

Ronnie's injured hand began to pulse more than ever, so he went to the bathroom to get a pain reliever and thought, even though he'd washed his wound thoroughly and doused it with antiseptic, it was probably time to change his bandage. Gingerly, Ronnie unwrapped the gauze, not relishing the thought of examining the injury, which had bled so profusely the day before. To his utter astonishment, the only blemishes on his hand were small white scars, barely visible. *How is this even possible? There isn't even a scab? And, if my hand has healed, why am I still feeling pain in it?* Although Ronnie couldn't be absolutely sure, the pattern appeared to resemble the bite of some animal. That's certainly what it had felt like when he had been attacked, but there had been nothing there except his charger. His charger! The last thing Ronnie recalled before he passed out was seeing it transporting itself on thin air, away and up the trail. He had blamed this fantastical mirage on his temporary shock from the injuries he had suffered to both his hand and head, but now....

Ronnie examined his hand again, replaying in his mind the panic of his workers, the shower of nuts on the roof of the trailer, and the rough pokes and prods he, himself, had encountered. "That's preposterous," he scoffed at himself in the mirror. "Invisible creatures? Get a grip on yourself, man!"

At that moment, a dim, long-submerged memory floated to the surface of Ronnie's mind. He must have been eight or nine-years-old at the time when Jim and he were sitting with other children at a church picnic. Great-uncle Will was telling them wild, fanciful tales about talking animals and the adventures he had claimed to have had with them. Everyone had listened closely, spellbound by the enchanting stories and always begging for more. "How did Will always end those tales?" Ronnie said aloud to his image in the mirror as he strained to recall. "What was it? Right on the tip of my tongue, tip of my tongue . . ." Like a single bolt of lightning shatters the darkness of the night sky, a flash of memory pierced his thoughts. "Yes! That's it! Will always claimed they were true! That's the day I got into that argument with Jim over it."

"Why does Uncle Will always say his stories are true?" Ronnie had asked Jim. "Everyone knows they're hogwash."

"I don't think so," Jim had answered. "I believe what my Grandpa says."

"Then you're a bigger fool than I thought," Ronnie had laughed and had shoved his cousin roughly. "He's a liar, flat out!"

"He is not!" Jim had fiercely insisted.

"Is too! Just ask anyone in the family. They'll tell you same as me."

Ronnie studied his face in the mirror once again. "Maybe you were wrong after all," he told himself, not without the awkward discomfort he always felt when having to admit to a mistake. "If those stories were all true, it explains what happened today at the site, and why Will held on to his land so stubbornly. He was protecting those critters." It was then a most devious and wicked idea took root in Ronnie's mind. He smiled gloatingly at his reflection, knowing exactly what action he would take in the morning. "Watch out, Jim," he hissed. "It's payback time."

***

Buddy and Sammy were in the den vigorously engaged in an X-box game when Ronnie stormed in. "Shut that crap off now!" he ordered fiercely.

Usually prone to argument, the boys responded to the urgency in their father's voice and, for once, complied with his command. "Where's the fire?" Buddy wanted to know as he hit the off button on the remote.

"I need you both to get your rifles out of the truck and clean them good. They have to be firing at their best," Ronnie told them.

"We're goin' huntin' now?" Sammy asked, glancing at his watch which indicated it was almost suppertime.

"Not now," Ronnie answered impatiently, "tomorrow, first thing, so no staying up until all hours like you've been doing this summer. I want you ready to go by 8 o'clock."

"What?" the boys exclaimed in unison.

"Isn't that just a little early?" Buddy asked.

"As far as I'm concerned," Ronnie replied, "it's not early enough. Now, get up and go get your guns like I told you to."

"Where are we gonna go hunting?" Sammy asked as he followed Buddy toward the doorway.

"Same place you went today," said Ronnie flatly.

The boys stopped dead in their tracks, their mouths wide with horror. "You mean we're going back to that haunted mountain?" Buddy was dumbfounded.

"I ain't goin' back there," Sammy declared. "No way!"

"You'll go, all right," their father threatened, "and it ain't haunted, so just get over it."

"Then how do you explain all the weird stuff that happened there today?" Buddy asked.

Ronnie smiled cruelly. "It's varmints," he told them. "Invisible varmints that are about to get the scare of their lives."

The brothers eyed each other nervously, both wondering if their father had actually lost his mind. "Uh, Dad," Buddy began hesitantly. "I hate to be the one to break it to you, but there's no such thing as invisible animals."

"On this mountain, there is," Ronnie responded matter-of-factly, "and we're gonna teach them a powerful lesson tomorrow. I guarantee they won't want to interfere with Ronnie Carson's plans ever again. Now, stop stalling and go get those guns!" He stalked off toward his bedroom to check out his own rifle and to make sure he had an ample supply of ammunition.

"Dad's lost it," Sammy asserted.

"Maybe he has," Buddy agreed, "but look on the bright side. At least we'll get some shooting in tomorrow."

***

"Dinner's ready!" Betty Rae hollered up the stairs to Ronnie.

"Not hungry!" Ronnie rudely retorted. "I'll eat later." Here and there, remnants of his earlier rage still plagued him, but the methodical routine of scrubbing the bore and polishing the barrel of his rifle was beginning to have its usual calming effect on him. As Ronnie wound down, his mind became clear and his thoughts rational. He was convinced there had to be a logical solution to the dilemma in which he now found himself. "Think, man, think," he exhorted himself. "There's an answer here somewhere, and you've got to find it quick. One way or another, you have to make legal claim to that land."

Ronnie put the finishing touches on his gun and propped it in a corner of the bedroom. Next, he opened his closet door and removed four boxes of ammunition from the shelves. "This should be plenty for tomorrow," he said assuredly, "but, to be on the safe side, I'll check each box to see if it's full." Ronnie placed them on the bed, opened the lids, and removed the bullet trays. To his delight, all the trays were full, their orderly rows reminding him of highly-trained infantry marching into battle. Impulsively, Ronnie plucked a bullet from its tray and cradled it in his hand. The casing, smooth and silver in color, was pleasantly cool to the touch. Ronnie liked the feel of it, the look of it, the way the last slanting rays of the setting sun embraced it, making it sparkle and shine. "You might look and feel pretty now," Ronnie addressed the innocuous bullet, "but you sure won't look or feel pretty to some critter tomorrow. I'll make sure of that."

He slipped it back into its place, and began packing the trays into their respective boxes. Then, Ronnie sat down in a comfortable chair by one of the bedroom windows and stared, unseeing, at the panoramic view spread before him. Slowly, but surely, the wheels in his mind began to turn as he contemplated his situation.

Meticulously, Ronnie reviewed each and every step he had taken to get to this point, and how, by backtracking, he could cover his movements and motives convincingly enough to have Will's property in his hands for good. Before he knew it, his head was filling with schemes faster than a creek swells in a downpour. A few phone calls, a few clandestine visits, a few more bribes, and everything should fall into place seamlessly.

A devious smile on his face, Ronnie took out his cell phone. "First call," he said, "goes to the lawyer. Peabody doesn't know who he is, so that's my safest move. We'll get that deed drawn up all tight and tidy, tight and tidy. No one will ever know the difference, and I'll be in the clear."

Once Ronnie successfully got the ball rolling with his instructions to Frank Thomas, his not-so-scrupulous attorney, he was feeling braver and more confident than ever. He was sure his plan would play out just as he wished it to. He was going to win this, and nobody would ever have an inkling of proof that what he was doing was illegal. "Not even, Jim," Ronnie said with smug satisfaction. "And you lousy, stinkin' varmints? You're history! You're about to find out the hard way that Ronnie Carson has the silver bullet, and I always win."

Chapter 7

Risk All to Save All

Ronnie, Buddy, and Sammy arrived at the abandoned and silent construction site at about nine in the morning. On their father's instruction, the brothers had loaded their backpacks with more ammunition than either of them thought they could possibly use up in one hunting trip. Ronnie had done the same with his and now hoisted it onto his back. "I know you boys think we've overstocked the ammo, but this ain't your ordinary hunt," Ronnie stated.

"What do you mean by that?" Buddy asked.

"I mean that all three of us are going to stick together going up that trail, and we're going to fire as many rounds in as many directions as possible."

"And what good is that going to do?" Sammy wondered.

"At the least, it should put the fear of God in these blasted critters," Ronnie told him. "At the most, we might just get lucky and hit one of them."

"Would that kill it, ya think?" Buddy asked as he fastened his water bottle to his belt.

"We can only hope," his father said through clenched teeth. "All right, let's move out." The trio headed across the gravel road, past the idle bulldozers and backhoes, and started up the trail. It was slow going, as they would stop every ten paces or so to empty another round into the brush, down the trail in front and in back of them, and even into the air. Unbeknownst to them, their mischief and mayhem was detected by Sharp-eyes, who was floating high above on the thermals. Knowing full well the consequences of being hit by a stray bullet, he sped on his agile wings directly to The Glade to warn the Old Ones of the impending danger. Upon reaching The Glade, the Red-shouldered hawk swooped through the Blessed Portal and hastened toward the Bell of Meeting. Gripping the rope in his beak, Sharp-eyes pulled on it furiously. Within minutes, all the Old Ones who had been in their Sanctuary chambers, gathered in the Banquet Hall, anxious to know why they had been summoned. Reverend and Mrs. Reverend were standing together on the High Table platform, as apprehensive as everyone else.

When she saw Sharp-eyes glide into the Banquet Hall, Mrs. Sharp-eyes flew speedily to take her place by his side on the platform. "What is it, my dear?" she whispered nervously.

"It's not good, my love," he said. "I'm just so relieved to find you here."

"What news, my friend?" Reverend addressed the hawk, his voice hushed and solemn when he saw the somber look on Sharp-eyes' face.

The hawk shook his head sadly. "Reverend, if you would be so kind as to focus everyone's attention toward me, I will tell you what I know."

The majestic Great-horned owl raised a massive wing and silence descended upon the assembly. "Honorable Old Ones," he announced, "please lend your ears to the news our companion, Sharp-eyes, brings to us today."

"How I wish with all my heart that my news was cause for rejoicing," the hawk began, "but, it is harsh to bear and even worse to tell. Ronnie and his two offspring are moving up our mountain trail with guns blazing, shooting randomly and frequently in every direction." There was a collective gasp in the hall as every Old One alike envisioned the probable tragedies left in the wake of this murderous spree. The wildlife on their mountain, protected from the hunter's gun for generations, would not associate the noise of the gunshots with danger. They could only pray no bullet would find an innocent victim and that, once the immediate threat had passed, they would be able to treat and heal any who were wounded.

"Indeed, this is a grave situation," Reverend declared. "Wily, who of the Old Ones is not in the Sanctuary at the present time?"

Wily, the red fox, was in charge of taking attendance whenever they gathered for a meeting so anyone missing could be apprised of what had taken place when they returned. "Racer and Mrs. Racer are not here," he regretfully reported, "nor are the Hoppers, sir."

"Who here knows of their current whereabouts?" the owl inquired.

Mrs. Cleverhands spoke up. "Racer is with Davy at the farm, and his missus is quite a distance east of here tending to a wounded squirrel."

"And Mr. and Mrs. Hopper went far afield to gather blueberries," Mrs. Smokey offered, "so they, too, are not in any immediate jeopardy."

"That is a relief, indeed," said Reverend. "Let us pray that they will hear the shots long before returning to The Glade, and use the gift of instant speed in doing so. As for the remainder of us, we are secure as long as we stay within the Sanctuary. I pronounce this meeting adjourned."

The Old Ones huddled in small groups throughout the hall, and some wandered off to other locales within their shelter, but all discussed the deadly seriousness of this situation. "But why are Ronnie and his sons committing such a heinous deed?" Mrs. Reverend asked in a tremulous voice.

"Revenge," Sharp-eyes answered tersely.

"Revenge?" Mrs. Reverend queried dubiously. "But, that would mean Ronnie *knows* about us or, at the very least, suspects that we exist."

"He knows from yesterday that *something* is in these woods," Reverend admitted. "We did run a great risk in utilizing the Tomato Plan, but I don't believe any of us felt we had another choice."

"We didn't," Wily stated, "and I, for one, am glad we took that risk."

"Hear, hear!" Mrs. Wily agreed.

"I don't think anyone regrets our actions," Reverend confirmed and turned toward his missus. "However, you raise a valid point, my darling. Ronnie heard Will's stories about us just as Jim did. To be sure, he dismissed them as sheer nonsense these many years. He must be livid with the loss of his would-be property, and such frustration can lead to irrational actions."

"And revenge," added Sharp-eyes glumly.

"Oh, I just dread the thought of what possible carnage awaits us when this attack is over," mourned Mrs. Wily.

Wily nuzzled her comfortingly. "We must pray, dear," he said, "and pray powerfully." As this small group bowed their heads in silent supplication, the same could be witnessed in many of the other clusters scattered throughout the Sanctuary. If ever there was a time to ask for deliverance, that time was now.

***

With his generous bulk, the exertion of trudging uphill, even with the frequent stops, was taking its toll on Ronnie. It was his sheer determination to even the score that drove him now. He halted to wipe the perspiration from his brow and reload his rifle.

"I'm getting bored with this," Sammy complained. "Can't we turn around now?"

"Shut up, boy, we ain't anywhere near done," Ronnie snapped at him. "We're going to reach the very top of this mountain before we even think about turning around, and then, we're going to keep shooting the whole way down."

"You're such a wimp," Buddy told Sammy. "I think this is fun. Wish I knew if I'd picked anything off yet, though."

"That don't matter," Ronnie said gruffly. "We're scaring the daylights out of them; I can feel it in my bones."

"Yeah, right," said Sammy sarcastically. "Invisible critters, my foot."

Ronnie dealt him a swift smack to the face. "You want to get sassy with me again? Do you? *Do* you?"

Sammy rubbed his stinging cheek. "No," he said sullenly.

"No, what?" Ronnie said, glaring at his son.

"No, sir," Sammy unwillingly corrected himself.

"Then shut your trap and keep shooting," Ronnie commanded. The three resumed their ascent, and Sammy decided, wisely, to keep his gripes to himself. They were closer to the crest of the mountain and The Glade than they realized at that moment. It was now about 11 o'clock, the time when, on the other side of this ridge near the foot of that same mountain, Davy, Anna and Racer were enjoying their picnic. Shots were flying thick and fast through the air, repeating rapidly like a string of firecrackers. When they reached the top at last, The Glade stretched before their eyes like a serene sea unaware of the impending storm.

"Will you look at this?" Ronnie said as they stopped once again to reload. "I never would have figured there was a glade way up here in the middle of the woods." He suddenly scowled as the slightest trace of a memory began to prick at his mind. *What is nagging me now?* Ronnie felt he should know, even if it was from long ago, just as he had recalled Will's stories the night before. He had the notion this recollection, whatever it might be, was somehow tied to those same stories, but it persisted in eluding him.

"This glade sure would make a great place for some cabins," Buddy observed, "don't you think, Dad?"

"It sure would," Ronnie agreed, though somewhat distractedly.

"I think it looks like one of those pictures you see in those dumb fairy tales Mom used to read to us," Sammy said.

"That's it!" Ronnie yelled so loudly, both boys jumped in surprise. "Well, butter my biscuit, boy, those are the first sensible words out of your mouth today!"

"What?" Sammy was understandably befuddled.

"Fairy tales, Sammy, fairy tales," Ronnie said, grinning ear to ear. "This here glade, you see, is where the varmints have their home. Yessiree! We've hit the jackpot now! Load them guns, boys, we're gonna have us a good long shooting spree!"

***

Beneath The Glade, secure in their Sanctuary, the Old Ones huddled together and listened in horror to the chaos unfolding above them. Though muffled, the sound of constant gun fire filled everyone with trepidation and fear for their absent companions and the unsuspecting wildlife that frequented this particular spot.

Mrs. Wily began to sniffle. "The foxes' den is so close to here," she cried. "What if one of those cubs gets curious about the noise and wanders from safety to see what it's all about? Oh, Wily, I can't bear the thought!"

"You must, dear," he told her, licking her stricken face comfortingly. "We all must. I promise, as soon as this nightmare is over, I will go with you to check on them." She nodded her head, but was too choked up to say anything else.

Just at that moment, a great murmur rippled through the hall as Racer, along with Mr. and Mrs. Hopper arrived, all breathing hard, and Mrs. Hopper's blueberry bucket trembling in her clenched paw. "You're back!" Prancer shouted joyfully. "You made it!" Delighted hurrahs and calls of "welcome back" resounded throughout the cavernous room as the three made their way toward Reverend and the Old Ones gathered around him. All had, thankfully, heard the gunshots from afar and knew, of course, their only option in returning safely to The Glade was to use instant transport.

"I had to make sure I had a reasonable estimate of where the shots were coming from before I could leave Davy and Anna," Racer explained. "By the time we made it down the trail to the meadow, I determined that their source was either in, or threateningly close to, The Glade."

"And we were headed back from the berry patch when we first heard the alarming noise," Hopper said. "Thanks to our sharp ears, we were warned in plenty of time."

"And I didn't spill one blueberry in getting here," Mrs. Hopper said proudly.

"I'm grateful for that!" Smokey declared, visibly relieved.

Everyone laughed at the bear's comment, and it felt so refreshing to assuage their anxiety with a moment of levity. Racer's face was the first one to lose its smile as he searched around frantically for Mrs. Racer. "Where is she? Where is my missus?" he asked in a panic. "Has she not returned?"

"No, my friend," said Reverend in a gentle tone which he hoped would calm the squirrel, "but I'm sure that she, too, will hear the commotion and arrive safely in our midst."

His words hadn't hung in the air for a second before Mrs. Racer, out of breath and obviously shaken, bounded into the room and, spying Racer in the crowd, hasted to his side. She gave him a grateful hug and kiss, and whispered, "I'm so glad to find you safe and sound, and none the worse for wear. I was so worried!"

"Worried? About yours truly?" Racer said with a bravado he didn't truly feel at the moment. "I've never met a bullet I couldn't dodge. You know that. I was worried about you, sweets."

"This is wonderful," Wily said with a huge sigh of relief. "All of us are finally present and accounted for. Now, if that ruckus above ground would cease and desist, maybe we could all return to a semblance of normalcy." Unfortunately, it would be a full hour before Wily's wish was granted. Even though time stood still within the Sanctuary, Reverend had been blessed with, among other gifts, an ability to sense the passage of time in the outside world, and informed the others accordingly. Sharp-eyes and Scout, the red-tailed and red-shouldered hawks, were pacing the floor anxiously, eager to be free to depart on a reconnaissance mission in order to assist the other Old Ones in locating any poor creatures that might have been injured in the deadly assault. While they waited, Reverend filled the Racers and the Hoppers in on all the details of this dreadful day.

"So you think Ronnie has determined we exist after all?" Racer asked, a concerned frown on his face.

"Yes," Reverend answered solemnly. "We've discussed it, and it seems to be the only logical conclusion to which we can come at this time. Ronnie is mightily enraged at being foiled in his land-grabbing scheme, and it seems to me that, as he, too, grew up hearing Will's stories, he took a gamble on believing the veracity of our dear friend for once."

Racer shook his head sorrowfully. "It was the Tomato Plan, wasn't it? That's what gave us away."

"Stop right now, Racer," Wily admonished him gently. "We'll have none of that."

"Wily's right," Hopper interjected. "Whether our actions tipped Ronnie off or not, I, for one, have never had so much fun in my life. You know, I pack a pretty hefty punch in these hind legs!"

"And from what I can tell," Wily said with a laugh, "you got them hopping. Get it? Hopping?"

"That's a good one, Wily, if I say so myself," the rabbit chuckled appreciatively.

"Okay, okay, enough with the fun and games, you two," Racer said in a serious tone, and turned toward Reverend. "So where do we go from here? I could tell Davy about this tragic incident, and he could tell Jim, but then how can Jim possibly prove Ronnie was trespassing without all of us having to come forward as witnesses? What would that ultimately do to our life in The Glade? Our safety?"

Upon hearing Racer's all too unsettling questions, every Old One grew quiet, and all eyes focused upon the owl, hoping for words of reassurance. Reverend surveyed them all slowly and deliberately, his face stoic. When at last he spoke, his answer was anything but the one they desired. Clearing his throat, as he always did, Reverend warned them somberly, "We may, my dear Old Ones, have to risk all to save all."

Chapter 8

Grandparents and Grand Pictures

When Davy returned to the kitchen, everyone, with the exception of Jim, was bustling with activity. Mom was brewing coffee; Mrs. Fairchild was trimming the stems of the wildflowers that Anna and Davy had collected, and arranging them in a vase; Mr. Fairchild was placing some heavy crockery on a high pantry shelf; and Anna, with Smokey and Mary by her side at the far end of the kitchen table, was busily drawing something. Davy approached Jim who was sitting as comfortably as was possible in the high-backed, leather office chair. "Feeling any better yet?" he asked.

"Not much, son," Jim admitted, forcing a smile. "I'm sure I'll feel some relief once the pain medicine kicks in."

"I'm sorry about your back, I really am," Davy said, patting his stepfather's hand in the same reassuring way that Racer often did his.

"I know you are, Davy, and I appreciate that," Jim said. "I'll probably be out of commission for the next several days. Can you help your mother with some of the chores I usually do?"

"Sure, I'd be glad to," Davy said, and truly meant it.

"Thanks, son," Jim said, wincing as he attempted to adjust himself in the chair. "I knew I could count on you."

Davy hesitated to ask the next question of Jim, but as busy as their lives had been since the moment they arrived, he felt if he didn't ask when he was thinking of it, he'd forget to ask altogether. "There's one more thing, Jim," Davy said. "When you're feeling up to it, could you give me a buzz cut, military style like yours? I'm tired of this long hair. It's way too hot in the summer."

"Sure can," Bob Fairchild piped up. "I know a thing or two about hair clippers and would be glad to cut your hair, Davy."

"You would?" Davy asked. "That would be awesome, Mr. Fairchild. I'll go get the clippers."

"They're in the bottom drawer of the dresser in our bedroom," Mom told him, and added, "I'll be so glad to see that unruly mop of hair go, that's for sure."

Davy retrieved them and ran back to the kitchen where Mom had already spread some old newspapers on the floor beneath a section of the bench. "You can sit here, Davy," she instructed him. "The paper will make cleanup a lot easier for me. But before Mr. Fairchild gets started, would you mind bringing in the clothes basket in from the yard? I forgot all about it."

"Well, well, Davy," Jim chuckled, "here's your first opportunity to fill my shoes."

Without hesitation, Davy handed the clippers to Mr. Fairchild to plug in, dashed outside to fetch the basket full of clothes, which was heavier and more awkward to lift than he had envisioned, and lugged it with great effort into the house. It was all he could do to lift it high enough to set it on the table. "Oh, thank you, sweetie," said Mom, planting a kiss on the top of Davy's head. "Ah! There's a farewell gesture to the impending loss of your locks. Go sit down and let Mr. Fairchild have at it."

"Here, Kate, let me help you with the clothes," Mrs. Fairchild offered. While the two women were sorting and folding the laundry, Bob got straight to work on Davy's hair. The feel of the clippers vibrating against his scalp made his skin tickle, but the boy held himself as still as he could. As the long, brown locks tumbled in clumps to the floor, Davy was amazed at how quickly the pile became mountainous. *Do I really have that much hair? Wow! I can't wait to see what I look like with almost none left at all.* The whole process, even the trimming, took no more than five minutes.

"You're done?" Davy asked in surprise when he heard Bob turn off the clippers.

"Yes, indeed," he answered. "Why don't you run to the mirror to see your new look, Davy, while I get this mess cleaned up for your mother."

"Yes, sir," Davy answered, swinging his legs carefully from his seat so as not to step on the hair that had been shorn from his head. "And thank you so much!

"Don't mention it," Bob said as he wrapped up the newspaper tidily and deposited it in the trash. He then poured four cups of coffee, placed them on the table, and rolled Jim to the head of it where he could reach his mug with ease. "Nothing like being waited on hand and foot now, is there?" Bob joked, his eyes twinkling.

"Oh, I don't know about that," Jim said wryly. "It's hard for me not to be up and doing things on my own."

"Well, my friend, I don't think that choice is available to you at the moment," Bob said, sitting down next to Jim and adding a generous dollop of milk to his own coffee. "When Susie's back went south last fall, I had the hardest time making her stay put. I'd say she's even more hard-headed than you are."

"What did you say about me, Bob?" Susie inquired, glancing up at him briefly as she continued her folding.

"I was just telling Jim here that I think you beat him out when it comes to being stubborn," he answered honestly.

"Stubborn? Me?" Susie protested in mock amazement. "Whatever would make you think that, darling?"

"Why, just the other day when I looked up 'stubborn' in the dictionary," Bob chuckled, "I saw your picture."

Everyone had a good laugh at this, especially Susie. "I have to admit," she confessed, "Bob's right about me being bull-headed. I was not at all a very patient patient when my back went out. Kate, you better hope Jim is more cooperative than I was."

"He will be," Kate said as she looked directly into Jim's eyes. "Won't you, honey?"

"Yes, dear," he answered in that singsong, teasing way of his.

This prompted another round of mirth among the adults. Davy arrived in the kitchen just in time to hear them and, though he had no idea what had amused them so, the sound of their shared laughter gave him a comfortable, warm feeling inside, just like family should. He suddenly recalled his wanting to ask Mr. and Mrs. Fairchild to be Anna's and his adopted grandparents, but he had neglected to tell his sister the plan. Quickly, Davy trotted over to her where she was still fully focused on her art, leaned down to whisper in her ear, and was thrilled with the look of delight that spread across Anna's face. "Let's ask now!" she insisted excitedly.

"Okay," Davy agreed, "you go sit beside Mrs. Fairchild, and I'll sit by Mr. Fairchild. Let me do the talking." The children eagerly took their appointed places with Anna promptly snuggling up to Mrs. Fairchild who reacted by putting a loving arm around the girl's shoulders. The men were talking, and Davy did not wish to interrupt them. He managed to make eye contact with Mom and tried to convey silently what he wished to do. She swiftly picked up on this, and when there was an appropriate pause in the conversation, she intervened.

"Excuse me, everyone," she said, "but, I think Davy has something to say or, to be more exact, to ask. Go ahead, honey."

Davy took a deep breath and plunged ahead. "Mr. and Mrs. Fairchild," he said, "Anna and I have something we want to ask you."

"Ask away," Bob encouraged.

"We were wondering," Davy said, "especially since we hardly ever see our own grandparents, if you would let us adopt you as grandparents. Would that be all right with you?"

Bob and Susie, understandably surprised by this touching invitation, looked first at each other, then at Jim and Kate who were both beaming their approval, and, lastly, at the wonderful children whom they already loved so dearly. "It would be an honor," Bob said in a voice choked with emotion as he hugged Davy.

Susie's smile through her tears spoke volumes. Anna hugged her tightly. "You'll be the best grandma ever," she declared.

Mom handed Susie a much-needed tissue and plucked another one for herself. "That is absolutely the sweetest thing anyone has ever asked us," Susie finally managed to say through her sniffles.

"There's only one problem," Davy confessed. "Now that you're our grandparents, it seems funny to call you 'Mr. and Mrs. Fairchild.'" What do you want us to call you?"

"Well," Bob suggested, "you could use the names our grandchild, Brian, uses."

"And what are those?" Anna asked.

"Bampa and Nana," said Susie.

"Sounds good to me," Davy told them. "What do you think, Anna?"

"It's good for me, too," she said.

"Then it's all settled," Bob proclaimed.

"My goodness," Susie said, "what an eventful two days these have been! All this joy and excitement is almost too good to be true."

"And I say we keep it going by having Bampa and Nana to dinner tonight," Mom suggested.

"Hooray!" Davy and Anna cheered.

"We'll accept on one condition," said Susie. "You let us make the dinner and bring it over so you can relax, Kate, and have time to tend to Jim."

"Are you sure you want to do that?" Mom asked.

"But of course," Susie declared. "How does homemade pizza sound to my new grandchildren?"

"That's my favorite," said Davy.

"Me, too," Anna chimed in, "but only if it doesn't have any toppings except cheese."

"I'll make a special, personal one just for you, Anna," her Nana assured her.

At that moment, the sound of Jim's unmistakable snore interjected itself into the conversation. Davy and Anna tried valiantly to stifle their giggles, and the adults immediately hushed their voices. "I guess the medicine is working," Susie whispered to Kate.

Bob and she got up quietly and tiptoed to the door. Kate followed behind them. "Thanks so much for everything," she said softly. "Poor Jim would still be lying on the lawn if you hadn't come to our aid."

"You're so very welcome," Susie said, giving Kate a quick hug. "Remember, keep the heating pad on him for as long as you can. We'll be back around 6:00, but call us if Jim needs Bob's help again."

"And," Bob added, "have that oven preheating to 425. We'll prepare everything, but we'll let Anna and Davy put on the toppings."

"Oh, they'll love that," Kate assured him. "See you soon, Nana and Bampa!" She closed the kitchen door as gently as she could and walked back to the table where both Davy and Anna were intently drawing and coloring. "What are you two making?" she asked.

"Get well cards for Jim," said Davy. "It was Anna's idea."

"No, it was Mary's," she corrected him.

"How sweet," Mom said. "He'll love those so much. When you finish them, put them on the table in front of Jim so they will be the first things he sees when he wakes up. When you're done with that, let's all sit and look at the pictures you took today. I'm anxious to see them."

"They're pretty good, Mom," Davy told her. "Thanks again for trusting me with the camera."

Mom gave him a sunny smile, and said, "It's easy to trust you these days, honey, and that makes me happier than you could ever imagine." She gathered up a stack of clean clothes. "I'm going to put these away and make up a pallet on the floor in our room for Jim to sleep on tonight," Mom told them.

"Why can't he sleep in the bed?" Anna asked.

"It would trouble his back too much," Mom replied. "He needs a firm, flat surface in order to get comfortable."

"Anna wrinkled her nose in distaste. "Ugh! That wouldn't be comfortable to me at all!"

"So, you wouldn't want to camp outside one night in our sleeping bags?" Davy inquired.

"That might be okay," she conceded, "as long as Racer or Mrs. Racer stayed with us. Then I wouldn't be afraid."

"I'm sure they would," Davy said. "Did I tell you Racer has a nest in one of the large oak trees by the porch?"

"Really? I thought he was always at The Glade at nighttime."

"Not always; he even spent the night at the foot of my cot one time."

"Wow! That's cool," said Anna, genuinely impressed. "I'm so glad Mary is with me every night. And now we have Smokey to keep us company. Thanks again, Davy. We really love him, and he says he loves being with us, too."

"I figured he would."

Anna cocked her head in an attempt to see what her brother was drawing for Jim. It was a depiction of the two of them engaged in target practice with Racer by their side. Impulsively, she asked, "Would you let me try your BB gun sometime?"

"I would," Davy said cautiously, "but it's sort of heavy to hold. It might be too much for you."

"I'm strong," Anna countered. "I bet I can handle it."

Davy doubted this, but not wishing to hurt his sister's feelings, simply said, "Why don't we leave that decision to Jim?"

Mom returned to the kitchen for another bundle of clothes. "Almost finished with those cards?" she asked.

"Almost," Anna said. "Are you, Davy?"

"Not quite, but getting there," he said, reaching for the colored pencils. "I just need to put some color on the picture."

For the next ten minutes, the two worked silently, concentrating on completing their cards before Jim woke up in order to surprise him. "Done!" Anna announced and held her card under Davy's nose. The boy was fittingly impressed with his sister's artwork. She had depicted Jim and her sitting in the living room armchair together with Mary and Smokey while he read them all a story. Her pencil lines were fine and detailed, much more so than his. She had even managed to produce some shading, which gave the drawing a three-dimensional feel.

"You really have talent, Anna," Davy said admiringly.

"That's what Mom and Mrs. Fairchild, oops, I mean, Nana, say."

"I guess it will take us a while to get used to calling them Bampa and Nana," Davy noted.

Anna got up from her seat as quietly as she could and crept over to Jim who, though not snoring quite so loudly, was still sound asleep. She placed her card in front of him, and then tiptoed off to locate Mom. Davy worked diligently to finish his card as fast as possible. He was looking forward to showing Mom the photos and was sure she must be done putting away laundry by now. Satisfied at last that his card was complete, though, he had to admit, it didn't look nearly as polished as Anna's, Davy laid it next to hers, and then retrieved the camera from the counter where he had placed it over two hours ago. Then, he, too, set out to track his mother down. He found her with Anna in the living room, seated on the enormous hearth of the fireplace, and joined them there.

"Good, you brought the camera," Mom said. "Is Jim still dozing?"

"Yep, but not snoring as much," Davy said with a smile.

"That's a relief," she chuckled. "Maybe he'll feel better when he wakes up."

"Do you think Jim will mind if we look at the photos without him?" Anna asked.

"Not at all," Mom reassured her. "It will give him something to do later in the day." She turned the camera on and pushed the button which allowed them to view the pictures. Davy had taken several with Racer in them, and he was curious to see if the squirrel's image could actually be captured, or if it remained just as invisible as it did to the rest of his family. Anna and he both leaned in closer for a better view of the tiny screen.

As she flipped through the photographs, Mom found something complimentary to say about each one. She was getting closer and closer to the shots of Racer, and Davy found himself holding his breath in anticipation. *Just one more to go. Please, please, let him be there!* To his utter delight, the next picture revealed a smiling Anna with Racer by her side, sporting his signature, lopsided grin for the camera. "Oh, Mom, I can't believe it!" Davy shouted. "It's Racer; he's in the photo! Can you see him?"

"No," said Anna, "I only see me."

Mom scrutinized the photo intently. It seemed to her that there was the faintest outline of a shadowy shape hovering next to her daughter. She tried holding the camera at different angles to see if it would become better focused, but to no avail. "What are you trying to do, Mom?" Davy wished to know.

"I don't see Racer," she said, "but I can tell there is something there. I just can't make it out."

"He's in some other photos we haven't looked at yet," he told her. "Let's keep going and, maybe, you'll have better luck with those."

"All right," she said doubtfully. The three scrolled through the remaining pictures with Davy pointing out the ones with Racer in them. Each time, Mom would study it meticulously, but could never see more than an indistinct shape. When they had viewed the last photo, she turned off the camera and heaved a sigh.

"Don't feel bad, Mom," Anna said comfortingly. "I can't see him at all."

Mom put her arm around Anna's shoulders. "I think I'd rather be in your boat, honey," she confessed. "It's more frustrating to know you see *something*, but can't make out what it is."

"Maybe," Davy suggested, "you have to believe before you can see Racer."

"What do you mean by that?" Mom asked, perplexed.

Davy proceeded to share with Anna and Mom what Grandpa Will had told him at the wedding reception months ago. He had not done so previously because he hadn't been certain at the time what Grandpa's words had meant; it had all been so mysterious and bewildering. Now, of course, having taken Will's place as the Chosen One, everything was as clear as crystal. Ever since Mom had responded to Prancer's spoken "thank you" that day, Davy had pondered whether she shared his gift, even if it was, as yet, undeveloped. "After all," he concluded, "I must have inherited this from someone, Mom. I think you have my gift, too. You just need to believe you have it."

"I'm not so sure, sweetie," she said hesitantly, "but I promise to leave myself more open to and aware of the things around me.

Maybe, just maybe, I'll grow into it. However," she added as she stood and stretched, "if I don't, I won't be any worse for wear." She handed the camera back to Davy. "I'm going to go check on Jim, kids. Do you think you two can entertain yourselves for a while?"

"Sure, can't we, Anna?" Davy asked.

"I think I'm going to read more of *The Lion, the Witch, and the Wardrobe*," she announced, hopping off the hearth and heading for the comfy chair in the living room where she had left the book yesterday.

"Don't you need Mary and Smokey first?" Davy wondered.

"No," Anna answered promptly, "they fell asleep about the same time Jim did, and I don't want to wake them from their naps."

"I see," he said. "Well, I think I'll take Maggie outside for a walk." Davy jumped off the hearth and trotted into the kitchen to see if Maggie was still there. As if the old dog had sensed Jim wasn't feeling well, she had curled up on the hard floor next to his chair where he continued to peacefully snooze. Mom was at the kitchen side table preparing to make a batch of brownies for dessert that evening. Davy bent down and stroked Maggie gently to wake her, and then motioned to her to accompany him. "Mom," he said softly, "I'm going to take Maggie outside for a bit."

"That sounds good," she said. "It'll do her good to stretch her legs."

"Oh, and Mom," he added, flashing a winning grin in her direction, "think about what I said, okay?"

"Okay, honey, I will," she promised as she returned his smile. Kate followed the boy and the dog to the kitchen door and watched through the window as the two strolled leisurely toward the apple orchard. "Believe," she whispered, echoing Davy's words from a few moments ago. "Believe...."

Chapter 9

A Boy Blames, a Man Claims

Davy and Maggie sauntered through the yard with its antiquated clothesline, past the hen house where the chickens were clucking contentedly, and on to the apple orchard which Davy had yet to explore. The trees were planted in two rows with twelve in each row. Their gnarly branches reached toward one another, forming a shady arch beneath which Davy and Maggie now walked. Though he knew next to nothing about plants, Davy guessed these apple trees were in their prime, as he could see countless clusters of developing fruits nestled among the leaves. He would have to ask his Bampa tonight at dinner, as the man was a seasoned horticulturalist. It surprised Davy that he so readily recalled this unwieldy word and even remembered what it meant but, then again, this first week at Grandpa Will's farm had been filled with nothing but surprises, the best he had ever known.

When they had spanned the entire length of the orchard, Davy could tell Maggie needed to rest. He chose a grassy spot beneath the last apple tree where the dog could doze, and he could marvel at the expansive meadow which spread before him, and the tree-covered mountains which rose up beyond it. The afternoon was warm, but there was a light breeze playing in the leaves above him. Their rustling whispers, as if they were sharing secrets, lulled him.

Davy stroked Maggie's silky head, which was resting on his lap, and immersed himself in the sprawling view before him. The tall grasses of the meadow, shimmering with various shades of green and gold, in the afternoon sun, reminded Davy of The Glade. Abruptly, he felt an overwhelming longing to return to that mystical, magical place, and to be surrounded by the Old Ones whom he had come to love so deeply. He thought of dear Racer and the gunshots the squirrel had heard earlier that day. *Had they, indeed, been coming from The Glade?* A shiver of dread coursed down Davy's spine. *What if Racer was hurt? Could that be why he had not returned this afternoon? Were the Old Ones in danger?*

Suddenly, Davy's mind was awhirl with anxious thoughts and horrific scenarios. Sensing his change of mood, Maggie lifted her head and whined at him. "I know, I know, old girl," he said. "I shouldn't let my imagination run away with me. I'm just worried about Racer and the others. Should I be?" Maggie thumped her tail in the grass and plopped her head again on his lap. "I guess that means they're okay, at least for now," Davy said, patting the dog gratefully.

Even though they could only converse verbally when Racer was around, Davy felt Maggie and he already understood each other perfectly. He relinquished his fears for the Old Ones, but there remained a nagging doubt in his mind that all was well at The Glade. As there was no way at the moment to know for sure, Davy decided he would have to be patient, a quality that he had not nurtured well in the past, and wait until Racer brought him the news.

The boy and the dog lingered companionably underneath the apple tree, and Davy allowed only good thoughts to enter his head. They might have stayed that way indefinitely had Davy's stomach not started rumbling. Lunch was a fading memory and supper seemed years away. "I need a snack," Davy announced to Maggie. "Let's go back to the house, and I'll give you a treat, too." The dog rose stiffly to her feet while Davy limberly leaped to his. Before turning to go, the boy scanned the meadow one last time, hoping for a glimpse of Racer bounding toward him, but the horizon was empty. Discouraged and hungry, Davy trudged back to the house with Maggie in tow. His disappointment must have shown on his face, as Mom noticed it the second he stepped through the door.

"What's the matter, sweetie?" she asked. She was sitting beside Jim's chair. He was awake now and, though not pain-free, was not in as much pain thanks to the medicine.

"Racer's not here," Davy answered glumly as he headed for the pantry for a granola bar and a bone for Maggie.

"Were you expecting him?" Jim inquired. "After all, he was with you all morning."

"I know," he said as he handed the bone to Maggie and reached into the refrigerator for the milk. "It's just this whole deal about the gunshots that has me worried."

"Gunshots? What gunshots?" Mom cried in alarm.

"The ones Racer heard earlier today when we were on our picnic," Davy replied. "I'm sorry, Mom, we were going to tell you, but then Jim hurt his back and I guess we just forgot."

"We?" Mom looked directly at Jim.

"Yes, 'we,' Kate," he said. "Davy told me as soon as he got back, but didn't want Anna to know about it."

"Racer didn't want her to know," Davy added. "He thought she would be too scared."

Mom sighed, "Yes, she probably would have been. That was thoughtful of Racer. Oh, I do hope he and the others are all right."

"They are," Davy assured her. "Maggie told me." Jim and Mom exchanged knowing glances. "But," the boy continued, "there's something else going on that's keeping Racer from coming here. I just wish I knew what that was." He took a long drink of milk and munched on the granola bar.

"I'm sure Racer or another Old One will come and tell you all about it as soon as possible, honey, so try not to fret about what might or might not be," Mom advised.

"Your mother is right, son," Jim said, and added with a smile. "And, by the way, I loved your card, Davy. It perked me right up."

"Good," said Davy, returning the smile. "Now, let's hope your back is ready for more target practice really soon. I miss it already!"

Jim started to laugh, but grimaced with fresh pain as his beleaguered back did not take kindly to that effort.

"Are you okay, honey?" Kate reached for Jim's hand. "Can I adjust the heating pad? Should I get you more medicine?"

"No, yes, and yes," Jim grunted through clenched teeth.

"Davy, fetch a glass of water for Jim so he can take his pills," Mom instructed while she carefully maneuvered the heating pad into an agreeable position. "There, is that more like it?" Jim nodded affirmatively. Mom retrieved the medicines from the buffet just as Davy handed the glass of water to his stepfather. Noting the concerned expression on the boy's face, Jim managed a brave smile, a word of thanks, and a heartening pat to Davy's shoulder. When Mom handed his the pills, he took them gratefully, drained the glass of water, and returned it to the boy's expectant hand.

"Now, that should help," Mom said with a smile, happy to see that Jim's face was again relaxed. "Is there anything else I can get for you?"

Jim thought for a moment. "Yes, there is," he said, "my Bible and my reading glasses."

"I'll get them," Davy offered as he placed the glass in the sink. "Where are they?"

"On the bedside table in our room," said Mom. "Thanks, sweetie!"

"And one more thing, Kate," Jim added with a sly grin as soon as Davy had disappeared down the hallway.

"What might that be?" she asked brightly.

"This," he said, gently guiding her face toward his until their lips met.

***

"Hi, Anna," Davy called to his sister as he trotted past her. She was still curled up in the armchair with her book and, he guessed, completely engrossed in the story, as she didn't even look up to acknowledge him. He shrugged it off and continued on to the bedroom. Once inside, he was struck again by the height of the bed resting in its gargantuan, antique wood frame. Its presence would have overwhelmed any smaller room, but here, it fit perfectly. It was, of course, neatly made with pillows plumped at the headboard. Mom was a stickler when it came to beds being made first thing in the morning. Davy remembered then that he had neglected to make his up today, and wondered if Mom had even noticed as she hadn't made any remarks about it. Then again, she had other things on her mind, what with his and sister's first solo adventure down the mountain trail and Jim's back failing him. He decided to go make it up as soon as he delivered the Bible to Jim.

The Bible and reading glasses were exactly where Mom said they would be. The book's cover, Davy noted, was soft and worn from use. Suddenly curious, he opened it to the place where Jim had inserted a needlework bookmark. Davy thought this a bit odd for a man's Bible until he studied it. On the cream-colored background of the bookmark was stitched a golden needle, a brilliantly blue spool of thread, and this inscription: "If your day is hemmed in prayer, it is less likely to become unraveled. Love, Grandma." *Well, that explains that.* Davy was about to put the bookmark back when a verse which Jim had highlighted caught his eye. It was

Psalm 138:7. Davy read it aloud. "Though I walk in the midst of trouble, you preserve my life; you stretch out your arm against the anger of my foes, with your right hand you save me."

Davy's brow puckered. *Why would Jim highlight this particular verse, I wonder?* He decided then and there to just come straight out and ask him. As he turned to go, there stood Anna in the doorway. "What are you doing?" she asked.

"Getting Jim's Bible for him."

"Oh, then he must be feeling better."

"Come with me and see for yourself," Davy said, and added without a trace of teasing in his voice. "By the way, Mary and Smokey are awake and missing you."

***

Jim turned the bookmark over lovingly in his hands. "Grandma gave this to me the same Christmas Grandpa gave me this Bible. The bookmark was stuck inside very much like you found it today, son. Typical teenager that I was, I definitely didn't appreciate these gifts at the time, and stashed both away in the bottom drawer of my dresser as soon as I got home. It wasn't until three years later, when I had enlisted in the Marines and was packing up my room, that I found them again, or, to be more precise, they found me."

"How can a Bible and a bookmark find anyone?" Anna wished to know. Davy instantly recalled what Racer said about the key to the box which held Grandpa's stories. It had wished only for him, Davy, to possess it. That was why Mom had never felt it in his pocket when she prepared the clothes for washing. *Grandpa's stories!* Now that The Naming was complete, he was free to read them whenever he wished. Davy was infused with a rush of excitement at the thought. *And I haven't even told Mom or Jim or Anna or the Fairchilds! But should I yet? I still want to ask Racer if it's okay. I wish he'd show up!*

"I needed them, Anna," Jim replied, "more than I knew at the time. I felt compelled to take them with me as if, by doing so, I could have Grandma and Grandpa right there with me no matter what happened out in, what was then, an unknown and intimidating world. Little did I know those lonely nights of reading and being reminded to pray would point me to the One who hadn't left my side for a single moment and who would always walk with me. The Lord knew my need before I knew how to ask."

Anna was smiling from ear to ear. "He knew mine, too!" she declared.

"He did? In what way, honey?" Mom asked her, a quizzical look on her face.

"When He gave me Mary," she replied, hugging the rag doll tightly. "I didn't ask for a friend or a doll, but I got both. Until I did, I didn't know I needed either one."

Now it was Mom's and Jim's turn to smile, and Davy found himself grinning right along with them. God certainly had given him, in the Old Ones, a gift for which he could never have dreamed of asking. Just a short week ago, he had not even known they existed. Now it seemed as if he had known them all his life. He thought, regrettably, about the boy he had been before arriving at Grandpa Will's farm, and how all that had changed the day he first met Racer. Davy was convinced the Old Ones were responsible for this miraculous transformation in him. As waves of gratitude washed over him, he was simultaneously convicted of the need to ask forgiveness from his family. The stark realization that he had never said an "I'm sorry" and truly meant it cut him to the quick. Tears sprang to his eyes before he could stop them.

"Davy, what's wrong?" Mom asked anxiously, placing her hands lovingly on his shoulders and peering into his face.

Davy's voice was so choked with emotion, he couldn't answer right away. He accepted a clean tissue from Mom's omnipresent stash, wiped his eyes, and blew his nose while his family patiently waited for an explanation. As Davy infrequently cried in front of anyone, let alone his family, he was sure they were all greatly perplexed by this rare episode. After sobbing for about a minute, although it seemed to him like hours, he gave another resounding blow of his nose and managed to pull himself together enough to deliver his message. "Mom, Jim, Anna," Davy croaked hoarsely, "I'm so sorry."

"Sorry?" Mom asked, her voice rife with concern. "What are you sorry about?"

Davy took a deep breath and allowed the words he knew he needed to say tumble out at last. "The rotten way I was and the rotten things I did and said to all of you before coming here. I was wrong, the things I did were wrong, and I never said I was sorry for any of it until now. Can you forgive me?"

In the stunned silence that ensued, the humming of the refrigerator sounded as loud as a freight train in Davy's ears. He studied each of their expressions: Mom's eyes swimming with tears, Jim's half-smile darting along his lips, and Anna's mouth agape with incredulity. Mom was the first to respond. She gathered Davy in her arms and held him so closely that, for a moment, he wasn't sure if he'd be able to breathe, but her embrace felt so good, he didn't care. He simply allowed her to hold him just as she had when he was little and craved the comfort only she could give him. Momentarily, Davy felt another pair of arms encircling his waist and Anna's head resting between his shoulder blades. Mary was pressed hard against his bellybutton. Confined to his chair, Jim was unable to participate in the group hug, but could acknowledge Davy's apology in words which, it seemed, had entirely escaped Mom and Anna.

"Son, I've had the pleasure of being proud of you this week for so many things," Jim confessed, "but none of those can hold a candle to what you found the courage to do just now."

Davy wriggled out of the dual embrace in order to wrap his arms around his stepfather's neck. "So you forgive me, too?" he whispered.

"Even before you apologized," Jim asserted, rubbing the boy's newly cropped head affectionately. "But i'm glad you decided to do the right thing." Davy pulled back from Jim so he could look him in the eyes. They exchanged warm smiles, which belied a new level of trust between them. "Remember, Davy," Jim spoke softly, "a boy blames, but a man claims. You're becoming one fine young man."

"I second that!" Mom exclaimed, finding her voice at last.

Davy let go of Jim, looked into his family's eyes, one face at a time, and said, "Thank you. I feel so much better now."

"And so you should," Mom told him. "There is nothing as sweet as forgiving and being forgiven unless it's knowing how infinitely God loves you."

"Amen!" Jim declared, thumping his fist on the table for emphasis.

Jim's "amen" reminded Davy to ask him about the underlined verse in the Psalms. "I know this is off the subject," he said, "but when I picked up your Bible, I noticed you had marked Psalm 138:7. Why is that?"

"I've highlighted lots of passages in this Bible, and for many different reasons," Jim explained. "This one, I recall, I read the evening before I was to be deployed overseas. As much training as we all had, I was pretty apprehensive about actually being in combat. This passage put my fears to rest because I could envision God's strong arm around me, protecting me from the enemy. And I knew that, whatever the outcome, nothing could separate me from Him.

"Weren't you even the least bit scared?" Davy wondered dubiously.

"Oh, there were certainly some scary times for me," Jim admitted, "but I found that, when they happened, I was able to face them."

"Mary and Smokey think you're brave," Anna declared. "So, do I."

"Do you now?" Jim said with a chuckle.

"Yes, we do," she answered primly, "and you've given me an idea for a new drawing." Anna flounced, her long braids swinging, to the other end of the long table where both children had left paper and pencils after making cards for Jim.

Mom, whose smile had yet to leave her face, reminded Anna to clean up after herself when she was through this time, then she turned to Davy. "And you, young man, forgot to make your bed up this morning," she said.

"I know, Mom, I'll do it right now."

"Military style," Jim added, his green eyes twinkling as he adjusted his reading glasses and opened his Bible.

"Yes, sir!" Davy saluted smartly, turned on his heel, and marched to the porch feeling lighter than air.

Chapter 10

Reverend's Choice

The Old Ones, clustered in their Sanctuary where time stood still, were not immune to the sounds made in the world above where time thrived and took its toll on all created things. To their utter dismay, the barrage of gunfire boomed above them for what Reverend estimated to be a good thirty minutes. They had even endured the ominous thuds of bullets hitting the stalwart granite rock above them, and hearts sank in the bleak realization that Ronnie suspected the whereabouts of their sacred abode. All eyes turned toward Reverend for a reassuring word or comforting glance, but neither was forthcoming. The owl's luminous eyes were closed and his noble, tawny head was bowed in silent prayer. The Old Ones, who had been praying aloud and, at times, loudly, took their cue from Reverend, and a hush fell over the Banquet Hall. The only sounds to be heard were the relentless rounds fired by Ronnie and his boys rampaging above them in The Glade.

Before he curtailed his chatter and bowed his head, Racer was growing more frenzied and agitated with every shot. At first, he doubted if the owl's course of action would help him, addicted to the spoken word as he was, but he was ready to give anything a try if it meant regaining the peace that daily dwelt within him, but now seemed unattainable. Racer breathed deeply, closed his eyes, and then allowed his breath to escape slowly and measuredly as he imagined emptying himself of every burden. Almost before he realized it, a soothing calm enveloped him and the din above faded into a distant echo. His breathing calmed as did the beats of his heart as Racer prayed wordlessly to the Creator, in whose arms he could always rest. A gentle paw slipped into his, and he didn't have to open his eyes to know it was Mrs. Racer. "This, too, shall pass," she whispered. *Yes, yes...this, too, shall pass.*

***

Ironically, it was Ronnie who initiated the ceasefire in The Glade. "All right, boys," he hollered at Buddy and Sammy, "that's enough huntin' for one day."

The brothers stared at their father in disbelief. Ronnie was alternately mopping perspiration from his forehead with a handkerchief and chugging water from his bottle. His shirt was soaked with ugly blotches of sweat. When he saw the way his sons were regarding him, Ronnie scowled so fiercely that the two actually cringed. "It's the damn heat," he declared and, letting fly a particularly offensive string of profanities, hoisted his rifle to his shoulder, and started back down the mountain.

Buddy looked at Sammy and rotated his index finger around his temple. "He's crazy for sure," Sammy hissed as they reluctantly trudged after their father at enough of a distance where their conversation would not be overheard. "We must have fired a thousand bullets, and not one thing to show for it."

"Yeah," Buddy agreed. "The old man has done some nutty things in the past, but this tops 'em all."

"You can say that again," Sammy muttered. "He ain't never complained about the heat before that I remember, do you?" Buddy frowned, trying to recall any similar gripes in the past. "I mean," Sammy continued, "every summer, we go to St. Simon's for vacation and it's hotter than blazes most times."

"Yeah, and Mom and Dad like nothin' better than to lie on the beach and bake," said Buddy. "I wonder if he's sick or somethin'."

"Sick in the head," Sammy stated flatly. "But we already knew that."

"No, I don't mean that kind of sick, stupid, I mean somethin' physical, like high blood pressure or heart trouble."

Sammy's eyes grew round with fear. "Y-y-you don't think he'll drop dead all of a sudden, do you?" he stammered.

Buddy halted abruptly and glared at his brother. "Since when do you care?"

"Since when do you?" Sammy retorted. "You're the one always back-talking Dad."

"Like you don't?" Buddy snorted indignantly.

"Not as bad as you."

"Yeah right, and pigs can fly."

"They can?"

"Sammy, you really are an idiot, you know th—" Buddy stopped mid-sentence. Though the air was warm, an icy chill spread through his veins. There, not thirty feet ahead of them on the trail, Ronnie lay, sprawled and motionless on the forest floor.

***

Reverend raised his head and blinked slowly as if he were emerging from a sweet, engaging dream. All around him, the Old Ones stood, heads bowed in prayer. As much as the owl loved the daily exchanges and conversations with his friends, he welcomed this moment of stillness. *Stillness?* In a joyful twinkling, Reverend realized the gunfire had ceased, and he sensed instinctively that Ronnie and his boys had retreated. A wave of relief swept over him and, however much he treasured the silence, he knew he must rouse the others at once to share this glorious news.

The owl stretched out his wings and flew soundlessly above the Old Ones, stirring the air just enough to coax them gently into the present moment. When he was satisfied everyone was focused enough to attend properly to what he had to say, Reverend cleared his throat, as he was ever inclined to do, and announced, "The danger has left The Glade! Let us rejoice and be glad!"

The Old Ones erupted into gleeful roars, which, after the intensity of the silence, resounded in the Banquet Hall like a thousand waves crashing upon the shore. Then everyone began talking at once, anxiously planning the next step that, though dreaded, must be followed if they had any hope of helping the creatures wounded in the brutal attack. Mrs. Wily began to weep anew at the thought of a precious fox cub having fallen victim to a bullet. Mrs. Racer tried to comfort her, but to no avail. "We simply must go now," the fox insisted through her tears, "I can bear this no longer!"

Overhearing her, Reverend swooped above the crowd and called for their attention once again. "We are all concerned as to what fate might have befallen the many creatures who dwell on our mountain, but we must be cautious. Sharp-eyes and Scout, would you be so gracious as to survey our surroundings before we depart? While I'm certain Ronnie is no longer in The Glade, we do need to see where he and the boys are on the mountain, and if, indeed, they are descending." With nods of consent, the two hawks sped out of the Banquet Hall, through the Blessed Portal, and into The Glade.

"Oh, I do hope they return quickly, and with good news," said Mrs. Wily.

"Yes," replied Mrs. Racer, kindly patting the fox's shoulder. "Good news is precisely what we need to hear right now."

Racer had followed the hawks to the edge of the portal, and was now pacing restlessly to and fro when Cleverhands approached him. "Shouldn't you be conserving your energy, my friend, instead of wasting it?" he asked.

"Couldn't sit still if I tried," Racer declared, a half-hearted smile on his face. "If I had known Ronnie would pull a stunt like this, I would have joined you in biting him the other day." Despite the soberness of their current situation, the squirrel and raccoon couldn't help but share a chuckle as they recalled the incident with Ronnie and the phone charger.

"Two bites wouldn't have made it any better or worse in the long run," Cleverhands observed. "I'm sure those punctures I made have all but healed already."

"Maybe not in the long run," Racer agreed, "but it certainly would have heightened the shock of the moment."

"Speaking of shock," the raccoon said, shading his eyes from the sunlight streaming in through the Blessed Portal, "the hawks have already returned!"

"What?" Racer asked incredulously. "How can this be?"

Scout and Sharp-eyes reentered the hall with such alacrity, Racer and Cleverhands were hard-pressed to scramble out of their way. The two headed directly for Reverend, exchanged brief words that no one else could hear, then all three rose on their powerful wings and vanished through the Blessed Portal, leaving a room full of stunned Old Ones in their wake.

***

"Dad!" Buddy yelled, dropping his gun and dashing down the trail toward Ronnie. "Dad!" Sammy stood as if frozen to the spot, silent tears streaming down his cheeks. Convinced that somehow the conversation Buddy and he had had just moments before had precipitated this calamity, he could not bring himself to draw one step closer. *Buddy is there. Buddy will tell me if he's alive or if he's....* The thought was too monstrous to bear and guilt, with all its deadly weight, plunged Sammy to his knees.

When Buddy reached Ronnie and saw the ashen face and slack jaw, he began to tremble, fearing the worse had, indeed, happened. Shaking all over and with tears in his eyes, the boy dropped to all fours and crawled the remaining few feet to reach his father's side. Gingerly, Buddy placed a quivering hand on Ronnie's chest. He was barely breathing, and the pulse of his heart felt weak and erratic. "Dad!" he called in desperation. "Dad, Dad, wake up! Don't leave us!"

Buddy was sobbing unabashedly now. Sammy, finding his feet at last, managed to stagger to his brother's side where both collapsed into the arms of grief. Their pitiful wails rose past the trees and on to the heavens, a discordant crescendo of utter despair and desolation.

"Dad, Dad, come back!"

"We're really sorry, Dad. Come back, please?"

"We'll be good, we promise."

"Wake up, Dad, please, please!"

Had their eyes not been so blurred by tears at the moment of their abysmal anguish, Buddy and Sammy would have seen the barest flush of color returning to Ronnie's face. Within the minute, his natural complexion was completely restored. Sammy, drying his eyes on his shirttail, was the first to witness this inexplicable and miraculous change, and hope infused the boy's heart. "Buddy, look! Look at Dad's face!" Sammy cried out, tears flowing anew, but this time for joy.

Hastily, Buddy wiped his eyes and gawked at the startling transformation before him. Hoping beyond hope, he once again tentatively placed his hand over his father's heart. Astoundingly, the beat was strong and sure, and the breathing, which had been so shallow, was now deep and relaxed as if Ronnie was simply sleeping. Dumbfounded, Buddy rocked back on his heels and let out a tremendous whistle.

"What happened, Buddy?" Sammy queried in a hushed voice. "Is Dad going to be okay?"

Buddy did not respond in kind, but glanced around curiously. "Do you smell honeysuckle?" he asked.

Sammy sniffed the air through his still stuffy nose. "Come to think of it, I do," he said, "but I don't see any around here. What does that have to do with Dad?"

"I don't know," Buddy admitted, his brow once again knitted in thought, "but I think we need to let him rest for a while." He reached toward his father's chest one more time just to reassure himself that all was truly well, and not a wishful figment of his imagination, when Ronnie's eyes fluttered open. Buddy emitted an involuntary shriek and jumped backwards, knocking Sammy, who was right behind him, to the ground.

"Ow!" Sammy hollered as his hind parts landed on a particularly unyielding slab of granite.

Ronnie sat bolt upright then, his eyes flashing and amazingly full of life. He surveyed his sons, noting that both bore traces of tears, which had left distinct rivulets on their grimy faces. Their expressions fluttered between stunned awe and genuine relief. Now they were both grinning broadly at their father. "Welcome back, Dad," Buddy spoke at last. "We thought you was a goner."

"You sure did look mighty bad when we found you here on the trail," Sammy added.

"And your face was all pasty grey. It was gross!"

"But now you seem to be your old self again."

"And that's good 'cause you scared us something fierce!"

As the boys prattled on, a bewildered Ronnie attempted to recall what had happened to him that would have made the boys think he was standing at death's door. He remembered feeling unusually overheated and fatigued as he lumbered down the mountain, and frustrated that the venture, at least in his mind, had been for naught. Try as he might, however, the memories between walking the trail and waking up refreshed escaped him. Buddy's voice interjected itself into Ronnie's thoughts. "We thought maybe you had a heart attack."

Ronnie found his voice and, in a few short moments, his sons would wish he hadn't. "Me? A heart attack? Rubbish! I've never felt better, never felt better. And, if I'd had a heart attack, I doubt I'd be sittin' up talkin' to the two of you right now, don't you think?"

"But we know what we saw," Buddy protested.

"You know what you think you saw," Ronnie corrected him. "I was tired and was far ahead of y'all, so I lay down for a minute. Guess I just fell asleep." Ronnie was no stranger to lies, but this time, as he honestly could not conjure up the missing memories, he concocted what he believed to be a plausible story. The boys weren't buying it.

"Look, Dad, I *do* know what I saw," Buddy insisted. "We both saw you smack flat on the ground like you'd been struck by lightning. You think we'd both have been crying if you'd only looked like you were sleeping?"

At that statement, Ronnie jumped to his feet and roughly grabbed the neck of Buddy's T-shirt. "What are you on, boy?" he growled just inches from the boy's face. "Come clean, now, y'hear?"

"I ain't on nothin', I swear!" Buddy protested vehemently. He knew his father had every right to be suspicious, as he had caught the boy smoking weed two months ago. After the thrashing and restrictions, Buddy had wisely decided to never try anything so reckless again.

"I don't believe you," Ronnie shouted, shaking his son as if he were a rag doll. "You tell me what you're on right now!"

"Dad, stop!" Sammy pleaded. "I saw you, too."

"So now you're sharing with your little brother, scum?" Enraged, Ronnie shoved Buddy away so violently, the boy fell hard on the ground. In an uncharacteristic gesture, Sammy hurried to his brother's side to help him up. "I've had enough of this nonsense," Ronnie continued. "Now go find your rifles and let's go. And not one more word, not one more word about what you worthless fools thought you saw!" With that, Ronnie scooped up his gun and stormed down the mountain, leaving his sons to wonder why they had wasted so many tears. In grabbing his rifle, had Ronnie's hand been just a half-inch shy of the barrel, he would have felt the silky softness of an owl feather.

***

When the owl and the hawks arrived at the scene, the piteous cries of Buddy and Sammy pierced the air and their hearts. Reverend landed beside Ronnie and scrutinized the man's face, one no longer crimson with rage, but sickly grey as the pall of death drew nigh. His sensitive hearing detected the faint beats of a failing heart. "Ronnie has suffered a heart attack," Reverend announced to his companions. "He is not going to make it unless I...." The owl's voice trailed off and his eyes closed as if he were deep in thought or prayer. Scout and Sharp-eyes exchanged quizzical looks.

"Begging your pardon, Reverend," Sharp-eyes whispered, "unless you do what?"

Reverend turned towards the hawks; his eyes, now open, were unwavering. "Unless I heal him," he stated firmly. "If I do not, Ronnie will surely die."

"Heal him?" the hawks gasped in unison, flabbergasted that the owl could or would even entertain such an outlandish notion.

"But Reverend, he's trying to kill us and everything living on this mountain!" Scout declared.

"Why in the name of the Creator would you want to heal someone who is our mortal enemy?" Sharp-eyes wondered.

"That is exactly why, Sharp-eyes," Reverend said gently and looked down at Ronnie sympathetically. "Our Creator placed us here to heal and help others. If I fail to aid this man, if I allow him to die right here and now, I have condemned his soul to be ever separated from the Creator." The hawks shuddered at that most ghastly thought. "His spiritual heart is as hard and as black as coal," continued Reverend, "and he believes that by giving more money than anyone else to the church, he has bought himself a ticket to Heaven. I have to heal his physical heart that he might have another chance at redemption."

Scout laid a wing on the owl's shoulder. "Reverend, tell us truthfully, do you really believe someone as wicked as Ronnie can repent?"

"Of course I do," Reverend asserted confidently. "It's his will to do so, which begs the question."

"Wait a minute," Sharp-eyes interrupted, "have you ever tried this sort of thing before, with a human, I mean? Do you have any idea how it will affect you?"

Reverend's voice was somber in his reply. "No, not to this physical extent," he admitted. The owl reflected briefly on how easy it had been to turn Davy's young and innocent heart around. Ronnie's was a completely different story. It was in that moment when Reverend acknowledged, in his own heart of hearts, he lacked the desire to heal this horrid man, even though he knew he must. Beyond a shadow of a doubt, he knew. He prayed fervently that his own divided heart would fuse in oneness with the Creator's will. *Not mine, but thy will be done.* Reverend then forced himself to gaze into the anxious eyes of his companions. "I think, my friends," he sighed, regarding them both as if it were to be his last moments with them on earth, "that it would be best if you stood each at one side of me as I attempt this. If I fall, I'd prefer to be caught before landing on Ronnie's chest."

Obediently, yet not without trepidation, Scout and Sharp-eyes positioned themselves to be at the ready to rescue Reverend should this impending feat turn out to be one of Herculean proportions. The owl took several deep and measured breaths, each one subsequently more expansive than the one before. When the hawks were convinced the owl could not possibly inhale any more without his lungs bursting, Reverend exhaled, and the air was instantly vibrant with the lush perfume of honeysuckle on a balmy summer's night. When the owl had expended all of his healing breath upon Ronnie, he lurched brutally backwards. It seemed to the hawks, who barely caught him in time, as if he had been struck down by an vicious, invisible force. Supporting him with their wings, the two dragged a limp and moaning Reverend away from the scene as fast as their clumsy gaits would allow. Spying a velvety patch of moss alongside the trail, they struggled toward it and laid the owl down as gently as they could. Neither said a word as they stood over their friend who, much to their consternation, was now emitting low and pathetically painful groans.

The shrieks and shouts of Ronnie's boys erupted so loudly and unexpectedly, Scout and Sharp-eyes leapt into the air with a flustered beating of wings. Within moments, they heard Ronnie's voice booming through the trees. "The healing was successful, it seems," Sharp-eyes noted gloomily.

"Yes," Scout acknowledged with a sad shake of his head, "but what about Reverend? What has this done to him?" He leaned his head down close to the owl's face. The faint aroma of honeysuckle still lingered there, but Reverend seemed to be barely breathing. The only assurance that he was alive was the distressing sounds he continued to utter, though these were growing weaker by the moment. "We must get Reverend back to The Glade immediately," Scout declared. "Sharp-eyes, help me get him to his feet so we can both wrap our wings tightly around him. He's unconscious, so he can be of no help with the instant transport."

Sharp-eyes promptly followed Scout's instructions, and, in moments, they had Reverend on his feet, supported by their strong wings. "Are you ready?" Scout asked Sharp-eyes.

"As ready as I'll ever be," he answered.

Scout took a deep breath, closed his eyes, and chanted:

Friend in peril,
Friend in need!
To The Glade,
We pray to speed.

To say that their arrival within the Banquet Hall generated pandemonium among the Old Ones would be a grave understatement. Seeing their stalwart, confident leader reduced to a semi-conscious heap of drooping feathers sent them into panic. The screams, the wails, the shouted questions soared to the rafters. Mrs. Reverend took one look at her beloved partner and fainted dead away. While Mrs. Hopper and Mrs. Silky rushed to her aid, Sharp-eyes soared above the crowd, just as Reverend always did, to secure their silence and attention. As they were so beside themselves, this took more effort than the hawk could have anticipated. When at last the noise subsided, punctuated only by muffled sobs and sniffles, Sharp-eyes addressed them. "The who, what, when, where, why can wait," he ordered. "Cleverhands, Racer, grab a large stretcher and place it next to Reverend." The raccoon and squirrel didn't hesitate for a second. This task was, at least, an easy one as the Old Ones already had stretchers in the hall, as they had readied them for the impending search and rescue. In seconds, they had located a suitable one and laid it next to their suffering friend.

"Now," Sharp-eyes continued, "as carefully as possible, roll Reverend onto the stretcher so we can carry him to his chambers. That's the way!" Racer and Cleverhands grunted with the effort of moving the owl, as he felt like dead weight beneath their paws. Prancer, seeing their predicament, hastened over to help, nudging at Reverend with his sturdy snout until the three succeeded in rolling the owl onto the stretcher. It didn't help matters that Reverend's moaning worsened during this process. It impaled anew their already broken hearts. When Sharp-eyes saw what a physical toll this had taken on the squirrel and raccoon, he knew they would not be able to carry the stretcher all the way to the owl's chamber.

"Silky! Builder!" he called. "You two take over the stretcher. Racer, run ahead and prepare a pallet on the floor since we can't lift him onto the bed. Mrs. Hopper, please brew some willow bark tea for the pain. Oh, superb! I see Mrs. Reverend is coming around."

Mrs. Silky and Mrs. Hopper were helping the poor owl rise to her still unsteady feet. "Don't think you should try flying any time soon," the otter advised her.

"No, no, I won't try to do that," Mrs. Reverend said, her voice barely above a whisper.

"Can you stand with just Mrs. Silky supporting you?" Mrs. Hopper asked. When the owl nodded weakly, she continued, "Good, because I'm going to make some willow bark tea for Reverend and some chamomile for you, my dear. Mrs. Silky will walk with you to your chambers, and I'll bring the tea in a twinkling." The rabbit turned and bounded off for the kitchen.

"He's in pain?" Mrs. Reverend gazed imploringly at the otter. "My beloved is in pain? What happened out there?"

"None of us know any more than you do," Mrs. Silky responded, "but I'm sure Scout and Sharp-eyes will tell you first.

Are you sure-taloned enough to attempt the walk to your chambers? They have already taken Reverend there."

"Yes, yes," the owl said determinedly. "I need to be with him."

***

By the time the otter and the owl wended their way through the maze of halls and at long last reached the chamber of Reverend and Mrs. Reverend, they realized that much had happened preceding their arrival. Reverend was seated on a palette laid adjacent to one wall, against which he was propped up and encased by generous cushions and pillows. Mrs. Racer was administering doses of willow bark tea into his beak with a medicine dropper. Although he had yet to open his eyes, Reverend was, thankfully, conscious enough to swallow the warm, soothing liquid. His moans were only intermittent now as the tea began to take effect.

Scout and Cleverhands were talking softly in a corner of the room, and Mrs. Hopper was just pouring a piping hot cup of chamomile tea as she had heard the owl and otter's approach. Sharp-eyes and Silky had rallied the remainder of the Old Ones to embark on their search and rescue mission, as The Glade and their mountain were no longer in jeopardy. Racer had given Mrs. Racer a whiskery kiss, assuring her he would to tend to any squirrels hurt in the melee, and urged her to stay with Reverend. "You're one of the best nurses we have, sweets, and you've taught me well," he told her. "Reverend needs you, and so does his missus. I'll be back before you know it."

"And will you be seeing Davy?" Mrs. Racer asked.

"Only if I have time," said Racer. "Let's pray that I do!"

When Scout spotted Mrs. Reverend entering the room, he hobbled to her side as quickly as he could and placed a comforting wing around her shoulders. "He's looking better already, now, isn't he?" the hawk remarked. Mrs. Reverend nodded, but her tears began to flow once more.

"There, there, dearie, it won't do him any good to hear you crying," said Mrs. Hopper, hastily bringing her the cup of tea. "Sit yourself down, get comfortable, and sip on this. It's good for what ails you."

Mrs. Reverend no longer had the energy to argue with anyone or anything. Although she was aching for Reverend and longing to know what had transpired on the mountain, she obediently followed Mrs. Hopper's advice. She felt the sooner she was calm, the sooner Scout would tell her of the events that had precipitated the condition her precious Reverend was presently in. By the time she sipped the last drop from her cup, she noted with relief that Mrs. Racer's ministrations seemed to have worked like a charm. Reverend was now dozing peacefully, and the distressing noises he had been making had ceased completely. "Thank you, Mrs. Racer," Mrs. Reverend said in a low voice, so as not to disturb Reverend. "You are a God-send."

Mrs. Racer smiled broadly at her. "It was and is my honor," she said. "Now, since Reverend seems at ease, I'll take these things back to the kitchen and see if I can be of any use to the others."

"And I shall accompany you to offer what help I can," said Cleverhands.

"Make that three," Mrs. Hopper chimed in, and added, "We'll return shortly to check on Reverend and you. Don't you worry, dearie!"

The three scurried out of the room leaving Scout, Mrs. Reverend, and the now blissfully resting Reverend to themselves. "They did that on purpose," Scout observed once they had departed.

"Yes, I know," said Mrs. Reverend, "so I could hear the story of what happened privately. So thoughtful, they are!" She turned to look Scout directly in the eyes. "Now, dear friend, tell me why Reverend is in this miserable state and spare no details."

Chapter 11

Made to Love and Serve

When the squirrel, raccoon, and rabbit entered the Banquet Hall, the first casualties had begun trickling in. There was a robin with a broken wing, a young squirrel with blood crusting along its back where a bullet had grazed it, and, as Mrs. Wily had feared, a fox cub with a mangled leg. The little creature was panting hard, her eyes glazed over with pain and fear.

Without a moment's hesitation, Mrs. Racer and Mrs. Hopper scrambled to gather ointments, salves, bandages, splints, and pain relievers to treat the innocent victims' wounds. Large bowls filled with water and clean towels had already been set out in the room by Builder and Mrs. Builder, the beavers. By the time Mrs. Hopper and Mrs. Racer returned, Cleverhands and Mrs. Cleverhands had adroitly cleaned the wounds of the fox cub and the squirrel. The robin, dazed and confused by its useless wing, which dragged on the floor, sat uncomplainingly waiting his turn.

"Here! Hand me a splint and some bandages," said Cleverhands when he saw the supply in Mrs. Racer's arms, "and something for pain. This poor bird is going to need it." The raccoon administered some willow bark tea to the robin who sipped it gratefully and promptly fell asleep. "Ah, that's convenient,"

Cleverhands remarked and wasted no time in setting the bird's fragile wing. "Yes," he whispered when the task was complete, "you rest now, little one. Your wing will be as good as new in no time."

"Mrs. Cleverhands! I need your help!" It was Mrs. Racer. She was hovering over the fox cub while Mrs. Hopper was treating the squirrel's wound with a soothing ointment to take away the sting. "Aside from being sore and stiff," the rabbit told him, "you have only a minor injury which will heal quickly. Here, dearie, drink this." The squirrel sniffed the willow bark tea and did as he was told. In moments, he was fast asleep.

When Mrs. Cleverhands reached Mrs. Racer's side, she could see that the fox was deeply under the influence of the pain-relieving tea. The squirrel had managed to stop the bleeding, but the bullet was still lodged in the cub's hind leg. "I can't remove it," Mrs. Racer said in frustration. "Your paws are so much more adept than mine. Could you try?"

"I'll see what I can do," Mrs. Cleverhands replied, not at all sure she would be successful. Like Cleverhands, she'd picked her share of locks over the years, but removing a bullet was an entirely different challenge. Carefully, she reached for the bullet, keeping her claws over it so their sharp nails would not inflict further pain on the already suffering cub. She then meticulously stretched her paw over the surface. Her claws, as they slid along the bullet's surface, helped to push the fox's muscle aside. When she thought she had a firm enough grip, Mrs. Cleverhands tightened her hold and pulled hard. Out popped the bullet, and the fox cub began to bleed profusely once again.

"Thank goodness you got it out!" Mrs. Racer exclaimed. "Poor wee lass is going to need stitches. I'll get right on that so I can be finished before she wakes up."

Disgusted and sickened by the bullet, Mrs. Cleverhands quickly dropped it onto a soiled cloth and proceeded to thoroughly scrub her paws. When she looked up, the next round of casualties was arriving. She heaved a heavy sigh. "Reverend sure chose the wrong day to be out of commission," she said softly. "We could surely use his gift of healing right about now."

***

When Scout finished recounting the unfortunate incidents that had taken place on the mountain, Mrs. Reverend wept quietly. Neither spoke for several minutes. Both focused on the slumbering owl whose chest rose and fell with normalcy as he breathed. It was Mrs. Reverend who broke the silence. "I understand why he did it, why he felt he had to save Ronnie," she said, "but will the others understand when they hear about it?"

"Provided it is explained to them the way in which I explained it to you," Scout assured her.

Mrs. Reverend shook her head. "They will be angry, Scout, especially if today's carnage is as horrendous as we anticipate it to be," she said mournfully.

"Angry? Maybe at first," he said, "but I know their love for Reverend and concern for his well-being will win the day."

"Speaking of well-being," she pondered, "I wonder how long it will take Reverend to recover fully from all this."

"As he admitted that he had never done anything to this extent before, I don't think any of us are capable of pinpointing that one."

"And that blow you described, Scout, what do you suppose that could have possibly been?"

"I've been ruminating over it since we returned," he said. "All I can think of is, when Reverend breathed life back into Ronnie, the transformation was so powerful that it sent an instant shock wave back at him."

"And never having tried such a feat before," Mrs. Reverend noted, "he was totally unprepared for such a reaction."

"So were we," Scout admitted. "We barely grabbed him before his head hit the ground."

"That's a mercy, indeed," said Mrs. Reverend. "Had Sharpeyes and you not been there, I shudder to think what could have happened."

"Where am I?" Reverend's weak, weary voice inquired.

"He's come around!" Mrs. Reverend exclaimed as Scout and she rushed to his side. "Oh, my love, you've returned to us! Thank the good Creator! You are in your own chambers, safe and sound."

"Chambers? How? Ronnie?" Reverend mumbled.

"It worked, Reverend," Scout said. "He's very much alive." The owl nodded almost imperceptibly and slipped into sleep once more.

"This is such a blessed relief," said Mrs. Reverend as she tenderly stroked Reverend's head with the tip of her wing. "Make haste, Scout. You must tell the Old Ones the good news!"

"That I shall, madam," Scout said with a quick bow, "but I will send one of them back to check on you both shortly."

"Yes, yes, that would be splendid. Thank you for everything, dear friend," she said, not taking her eyes off the snoozing Reverend.

"You are most welcome," said Scout as he exited the chamber and hurried as fast as possible down the long and twisting corridors leading to the Banquet Hall. When he turned the last corner, chaos greeted him. Forest creatures of every description and in various stages of treatment and recovery lay on makeshift pallets strewn on the stone floor. Old Ones were hustling to and fro amidst the patients, seeing to the needs of each the best they could. Others were bringing in the wounded on stretchers, depositing them as gently as possible on a quilt or blanket, and racing out again in the desperate search for more victims.

As there was no sign of Mrs. Scout or the other hawks, Scout surmised they must still be needed in the rescue efforts. The number of casualties who had hope of healing made him wonder morbidly how many more lay lifeless on the forest floor. He knew their bodies would be lovingly gathered up and taken to the Place of Burial where the Old Ones with a propensity for digging would, he supposed, already be hard at work. Prayers would be offered for each creature's soul as the shell of bone and fur or feathers that had once contained it were laid to rest. Scout closed his eyes and prayed silently for the wounded and the dead, and for the Old Ones to understand Reverend's rational for healing the very man who had perpetrated these heinous deeds. *Reverend! I must tell the others!*

Just as Sharp-eyes had done earlier that same day, Scout shot into the air and flew in circles above them until they grew quiet in anticipation of an important announcement. "My friends," Scout began, "I bring you hope in the midst of this tragic day. Reverend has come around at last!"

As weary and stressed as they were, the Old Ones cheered and hugged one another for joy. "Is he well enough to lend us a hand here?" Cleverhands shouted above the clamor.

Scout descended and stood next to the raccoon. "Not quite yet, I'm afraid," the hawk answered stoically, "but at least he is resting comfortably."

"It's not as if we can't treat the wounded with our own skills," said Cleverhands, "but Reverend's gift of healing would certainly hurry things along." Scout winced involuntarily at this remark, recalling the tremendous effort it had required on the owl's part to accomplish Ronnie's recovery, and certain that it would take hours, maybe days spent in the Sanctuary, before Reverend would have sufficient strength to employ that gift again. The hawk's unusual reaction had not gone unnoticed by the raccoon. "What's the matter? Did I say something wrong?"

Scout simply shook his head, but there was no mistaking the hint of sadness in his eyes. Cleverhands' own eyes narrowed as he leaned in closer to the hawk and dropped his voice to a whisper. "You're holding out on me, aren't you?" he said accusingly. "I know that something terrible happened to Reverend today when you were with him. So are you going to tell me about it or not?"

"Not," was Scout's terse answer.

"Not?" Cleverhands was taken aback.

"This is neither the time nor the place," said the hawk, flapping his wings and rising into the air. "You have work to do, more, I dare say, than you would like, and I, too, have urgent business to attend to." With that remark, Scout was off to fetch an Old One to tend to the needs of Mrs. Reverend, and to lend his expertise, too long delayed, in the search and rescue mission.

He left in his wake a stunned and bewildered Cleverhands. "What bee got in his bonnet, I wonder?" he muttered to himself, but was not afforded the luxury to reflect upon what had just transpired between them.

"Emergency! Emergency!" Prancer bellowed as he entered the hall. A stretcher had been harnessed like a travois behind him. On it lay and elegant doe, her tawny flank stained with blood, the light in her liquid brown eyes fading by the moment. A whimpering fawn with Mrs. Prancer by his side had followed them all the way from the thicket where they had been secluded and sleeping when a stray bullet shattered their lives.

Cleverhands and Mrs. Racer dashed over to them. It didn't take more than the usual amount of time to assess the seriousness of the doe's injury. "Mrs. Racer, unfasten the harness from the stretcher," the raccoon ordered. "It's too risky to try and roll her onto a pallet." The squirrel hurriedly complied and, with Mrs. Cleverhands' assistance, joined Cleverhands, who was doing what he could to staunch the bleeding. The stretcher was already soaked in crimson. Mrs. Racer gently lifted the doe's head and attempted to give her a generous dose of willow bark tea. When she saw most of it dribbling back out of the doe's mouth, the squirrel was beside herself.

"Fresh water! Clean towels!" Cleverhands barked. Builder and Mrs. Builder waddled as quickly as they could to deliver the supplies that the raccoon had requested. The two had been emptying and refilling pans and buckets of water, and washing out the stained cloths all afternoon. They went about these chores cheerfully and tirelessly, inspiring others with their relentless spirits. The two embodied the phrase "busy as a beaver," and the Old Ones were never more thankful for their hard work than they were today.

Determined to remove the fawn from the grisly scene in the hall, Mrs. Prancer coaxed him to accompany her down the hallway that led to the chamber she shared with Prancer. The pitiful thing was reluctant to leave his mother, but with head hanging woefully, he finally allowed himself to be led away by this kindly doe who was twice the size of any he had ever seen. When they reached the chambers, Mrs. Prancer motioned toward some plush cushions on the floor where the fawn could lay down. He didn't hesitate a moment to accept this invitation. His legs were weak and wobbly from the long walk, and he was relieved to rest them.

To his surprise, the cushions smelled like sweet grass and were just as springy beneath him. The biggest surprise of all, though, was the odd-looking contraption with a rubber tip and filled with white liquid, which Mrs. Prancer seemed to have produced out of nowhere. She set it down right at the fawn's head so his mouth could easily reach it. She couldn't help but chuckle as she watched him sniff the tip tentatively and then, with eyes full of wonder as he realized what was inside, latch onto the tip to savor some fresh, delicious milk. "That's right, little lad," Mrs. Prancer said lovingly, "we must keep you strong and healthy for your mother's sake and for yours."

The thought of the doe's plight brought tears to her eyes. She couldn't abide the thought that the fawn could be orphaned this very day. Mrs. Prancer fervently hoped they had gotten to the doe in time, and recalled thankfully that had it not been for Mrs. Sharp-eyes who had spied the fawn's movement in the thicket, they would have missed her altogether. The hawks' assistance had been immeasurable today. *But I don't recall seeing Scout.* It suddenly dawned on her that he must have stayed behind with Reverend. A stab of guilt made her flinch. Mrs. Prancer had been so consumed by the demands of the rescue mission, she hadn't entertained one thought about the dear owl or his condition. She prayed now for Reverend to be on the mend, and hoped if Prancer heard any news, he would come tell her right away.

The anxious bleats of the fawn refocused her attention. With his stomach full and satisfied, he was ready to nap, but his mother was not there to snuggle with him and keep him warm. Mrs. Prancer knew just what to do. She nuzzled the fawn to calm him down and then lay down behind him so he could slumber securely by her side. This arrangement suited the fawn perfectly, and he was soon fast asleep. His relaxed and rhythmic breathing was like a tonic to his surrogate mother. Mrs. Prancer burrowed her head in the soft cushions, closed her eyes, and lapsed willingly into the land of dreams.

***

In the Banquet Hall turned hospital, the Old Ones continued to toil ceaselessly in tending to their patients. The once steady stream of casualties had mercifully dwindled by mid-afternoon, and those who had been involved in their rescue were wearily returning to the Sanctuary. Mrs. Hopper and Mrs. Builder had prepared much needed refreshments for everyone. This nourished them in both body and spirit. The addition of extra paws to aid in treating the injured allowed Cleverhands and Mrs. Racer to take a much-warranted break from their labors.

The raccoon yawned broadly, "I am worn out," he declared. "If I am going to be of any use later this evening, I think it best to take a nap. Mrs. Cleverhands has already retired for the time being."

"That's a good idea," Mrs. Racer concurred. "First, though, I'm going to check on Mrs. Reverend and give Mrs. Whiskers a break."

As they trotted off to their separate destinations, Mrs. Racer noted that Racer was not among the Old Ones who had recently returned. *He must be with Davy. Oh, I wonder how the dear child will take the disastrous news?* She knew Racer would break it to him as gently as possible, and remain with the boy as long as he must to offer comfort and reassurance, even if it meant spending the night at the farmhouse. She always missed Racer when they were apart, but understood fully that serving and loving others often called them away from each other. *And that's what we were created to do. We were made to love and serve.* That thought was as heartening as Racer's grin, and Mrs. Racer found herself smiling in spite of the sorrow that had permeated the day. She was still sporting this expression as she approached the owls' chamber and knocked briskly on the half-opened door.

"Come in," Mrs. Whiskers said invitingly in her high-pitched voice which always reminded Mrs. Racer of tinkling wind chimes.

"Well, you must have some good news to share, judging by that smile on your face," Mrs. Reverend observed as the squirrel bounded into the room.

"In all honesty, no," Mrs. Racer confessed. "The situation in the Banquet Hall is the polar opposite of happy, as I'm sure Mrs. Whiskers has already told you, and everyone is nigh exhausted. However, it dawned on me just moments ago that, as tragic as it is, we are here to help, doing precisely what we were intended for, and that thought filled me with a joy I never imagined I could feel on a day like today."

Mrs. Reverend stretched out one wing and engulfed the squirrel in a side embrace. There were tears in her eyes, but they were anything but sad. "How right you are," she whispered hoarsely. "No matter what the trials of the moment may be, we cannot lose sight of the larger picture. Thank you, dear friend, for reminding us of that." The owl looked over her shoulder at Reverend, who was still slumbering, and hung her head in shame. "I'm afraid I couldn't see that bigger picture today when Reverend was enduring such pain and suffering."

"Now, now," Mrs. Whiskers admonished, "we'll have none of that. You were in shock, for goodness sake. If it had been Whiskers, I would have reacted exactly as you did, and that's the truth."

"As would I," Mrs. Racer assured her and nodded toward Reverend. "Has he awakened at all since Scout informed us he'd come around?"

"Just a bit of murmuring here and there," Mrs. Reverend answered, "unintelligible as far as I can tell, but I'm taking that as a good sign."

"And so, you should," said the squirrel. "Now, I came to see if you needed anything to eat or drink or, if you, Mrs. Whiskers, needed me to stay with Mrs. Reverend for a while?"

"I tell you what," the mouse suggested, "why not allow me to procure refreshments while you stay here and get some rest. You've truly been overworked today."

"A marvelous gesture, Mrs. Whiskers," said Mrs. Reverend.

"I must admit I am just a wee bit tired," Mrs. Racer confessed.

"Then it's all settled," said Mrs. Whiskers as she scurried toward the door. "I'll return in no time." Had the mouse been clairvoyant, she would never have abandoned her friends at that moment.

Chapter 12

In the Midst of Trouble

Mrs. Prancer woke with a start and sensed immediately that something was amiss. The air in the room felt hot and close, as it does right before an impending thunderstorm, and there was a repugnant odor to it, the likes of which she had never smelled before. Cautiously, so as not to disturb the fawn, she rose to her feet and tiptoed to the door, which she had left ajar. When she poked her head into the hallway, the air became even thicker and the stench heavier. Her pulse quickened and her limbs tensed as an unnamed fear welled within her. She longed for Prancer's company and reassurance, but to seek him out would mean abandoning her charge.

Mrs. Prancer glanced nervously over her shoulder only to find that the fawn continued to sleep soundly, seemingly unaffected by the ominous atmosphere pervading the Sanctuary. The hallway, usually bustling with activity as the Old Ones moved to and from their chambers, was eerily silent, so hushed that the sound of her own breathing startled her. The doe swiveled her ears, straining to hear any hint of a footfall or a friendly voice, but the hall remained as silent as a tomb.

Trembling all over and feeling nauseated by the ghastly smell, Mrs. Prancer was just about to retreat to her room when she heard the unmistakable, though faint, clatter of hooves on the stone floor of the hall. *Prancer!* He was coming at a gallop and, as he did, the hoof beats shattered the stillness as if a hundred drums were being hammered at once. The buck emerged around the corner of the hallway at full tilt, his eyes wild with urgency. The sight of him in such a state dashed all hopes of comfort now. Mrs. Prancer knew he would not, could not, stop. "It's Reverend!" he shouted as he neared, then passed her at lightning speed. "No time to lose!"

Her dread deepened as she watched him round another bend and listened to his hoof beats transform from kettle drum, to bass, to snare, and then vanish altogether. Once again, the palpable silence of the hallway closed in on her, and she felt shaken to the core of her soul. "Reverend," Mrs. Prancer whispered, striving to quell the panic that threatened to overtake her. "I must go see him, must see for myself, and help if I can." Again, she checked to make sure the fawn was still resting and, mouthing a prayer for the little lad and his mother, stealthily shut the door for his safety, and set out in the direction from which Prancer had come, praying for the dear owl with every breath.

***

Davy tucked in the last corner on his cot and plumped his pillow the way he had seen Mom do it hundreds of times. He stood back to admire his work, gave himself a thumbs-up, and squatted down by Maggie, who was sprawled on her bed, so he could stroke her side. Davy was still getting used to the idea of having a dog and was sure he would never tire of how warm and soft her fur felt beneath his palm. As supple as Maggie's coat was, however, it couldn't hold a candle to the glory that was Racer's. Its velvety texture defied description, and Davy smiled blissfully as he recollected the first time he touched it. In contrast to his marvelous fur, Racer's whiskers were tough and wiry, and had pricked, or tickled, the boy's face every time the squirrel had planted a kiss there. Davy's smile faded as quickly as it had come. *Where are you, Racer? Where are you?*

He gazed across the garden and the meadow to the mountains beyond. His eyes searched high and low for any sign of his friend, but except for the occasional bird soaring heavenward, there was no other discernible movement. Davy heaved a disappointed sigh and, as if in empathy, Maggie breathed one, too. "You miss Racer, too, don't you, girl?" The dog thumped her tail twice on the floor. This small sign of affirmation restored Davy's spirits. He sat comfortably next to her, and continued to pat her as he drank in the scenery, which calmed him now just as it had earlier in the day. *Is this what Mom means when she says she needs her quiet time? Do I need it, too? Does everybody?*

Davy closed his eyes for a moment, needing to digest these fresh thoughts while his mind, seemingly unbidden, searched for something else, something deeply hidden, something, he knew intuitively was the connecting piece in this puzzle. At home in the city, there had always been noise surrounding him – television, computer games, radio, traffic rumbling in its continual flow, but here on the farm, the peacefulness was so complete, even the chirping of a bird or the sighing of the wind in the leaves could startle him. The dearth of sound was, in a way, a sound in itself, as Davy found himself listening more intently and intentionally to the silence. If anyone had told him a short week ago that he would enjoy such a moment as this, he would have insisted they were out of their minds. Yet here he was, not just enjoying it, but reveling in it. *But why? Why does this make me feel so good inside?*

Maggie's stirring beneath his hand roused Davy from his reverie. She had raised her head, her eyes alert, her moist, black nose twitching furiously. "What is it, Maggie?" he asked. "What do you smell?" The dog emitted a mournful howl that made the hair rise on Davy's neck. He scrambled to his feet and frantically searched the landscape, hoping to discover what was upsetting Maggie so. She howled again, stumbled to her feet, and began pacing the floor restlessly.

Mom's troubled face appeared abruptly at the door. "Davy, what in the world is wrong with Maggie?"

"I don't know, Mom," he said, his expression mirroring hers. "One minute she was perfectly calm and the next she was sniffing the air and howling at who knows what. I can't see anything out there that would upset her."

Mom approached him and placed an arm around his shoulder. "Maybe," she said, "Maggie smells or senses something we can't."

The dog began whining agitatedly as she patrolled the porch, her eyes ever focused on a spot on the horizon where nothing out of the ordinary was visible. "Whatever it is," Davy said gloomily, "it can't be good."

"Now, Davy," Mom chided, "there you go assuming the worst again. She probably picked up the scent of a wild animal she's not particularly fond of and that's got her riled. Remember, we're just getting to know Maggie and her quirks. This may be one of them."

Davy wished with all his heart that Mom was right, but the gnawing unease he felt as he observed the dog's odd behavior would not allow him to believe her. With every passing moment, he became more convinced Maggie was reacting to something awful that had, or was about to, happen. *If only you could talk to me. Racer, where are you when I need you?* Instantly, Davy was plunged from anxiety into bleak despair as he sensed his earlier fears materializing into reality. *The Old Ones are in danger!*

***

With every step she took, it seemed to Mrs. Prancer that the air became heavier and hotter, and the odor more putrid. Its stench made her gag and cough, but she kept on even though the heat made her think the very walls were closing in on her. If this wasn't unsettling enough, her sharp ears detected a doleful moan, which rose and fell repeatedly, growing ever louder the closer she came to the Reverend's chambers. The doe's breathing became labored in the foul air, and she slowed her gait in the hope it would help. The passageways of her nose and throat felt raw as if they had been scorched by boiling water, and her eyes were stinging so painfully, she could barely hold them open.

Because of these afflictions, Mrs. Prancer became a bit disoriented and was genuinely surprised when she turned the next corner and realized the owls' chamber, with its door opened wide, was only moments away. Determined, she broke into a trot, but stopped dead in her tracks when the moans escalated to a harrowing wail and climaxed in a blood-curdling screech that reverberated throughout the corridor in a hideous crescendo. Quivering all over, Mrs. Prancer waited for the last remnant of the unearthly noise to abate before she took another step on legs she was certain had turned to rubber. It took every ounce of the noble doe's courage to proceed to her destination, dreading the horrific scene that must lie ahead, but no amount of imagination could ever have prepared her for what met her eyes.

Mrs. Reverend and Mrs. Racer were huddled together and trembling in the corner of the room closest to the door. Both had handkerchiefs draped over their noses and mouths, and Mrs. Reverend was crying uncontrollably. On the far side of the room, thrashing wildly about on the floor, his pillows in unsightly disarray, was an unrecognizable Reverend. Mrs. Prancer stared at him in what could only be deemed morbid fascination. His feathers, always elegantly smooth from conscientious preening, were now standing on end as if each quill was a dagger piercing the owl's body. His wings flapped erratically as if attached to strings pulled mercilessly by a deranged puppeteer. His majestic beak was open and twisted askance as the endless moans and senseless verbiage spilled forth. But it was Reverend's eyes, once so warmly amber and genial, windows to the owl's great soul, which alarmed Mrs. Prancer the most and drove her to the depths of anguish. The dark pupils were so dilated, they threatened to engulf the entire iris and, in the middle of them where the normal pupil should have been, sinister, crimson slits had appeared. They held the doe's gaze despite her crumbling will to turn away. She felt her blood turning to ice in her veins.

"Don't look at them!" Mrs. Racer screamed as she leapt upon Mrs. Prancer's back and tossed a large handkerchief over the doe's eyes and nose. The cloth was heavily scented with lemon verbena which instantly soothed her tender, aching throat. More importantly, it broke the wicked spell into which she had been inexplicitly drawn.

Mrs. Prancer exhaled mightily with relief. "Thank you, my friend," she whispered to the squirrel.

Mrs. Racer patted the doe's neck reassuringly. "Look to your left and I'll drop the handkerchief from your eyes," she said. Mrs. Prancer did so most willingly, and both quickly retreated in the direction of Mrs. Reverend who, by this time, was completely beside herself.

"I can't bear to be here and I can't bear to leave him," she sobbed, leaning against the doe's shoulder for solace.

"But I don't understand," said Mrs. Prancer. Her voice was shaking so, she hardly recognized it. "What happened to Reverend? Is he...." An ungodly groan arched into an appalling screech, drowning out her words. If this weren't enough to cower the three already cringing in the corner, the vile string of profanities, harsh and guttural, which ensued would have reduced the bravest of Old Ones to unspeakable terror.

"Stop resisting me!" Reverend growled in a chillingly demonic tone. "You cannot win. You cannot win. You cannot win."

"Leave me," Reverend gasped weakly in his own comforting voice. "I command you: Leave me! Oh, where is Davy? Chosen One...Chosen One...."

The utterance catapulted Mrs. Reverend into a fresh round of weeping. Mrs. Prancer was aghast. The reeking air, the diabolical oaths, and the gruesome screams converged into one unthinkable admission: evil had entered the Sanctuary; Reverend was possessed.

***

Abruptly, Maggie ceased her striding and sat down right in front of the screen door, eyes fixed on some distant object that Davy, as of yet, was unable to see. He walked over to the dog and stood behind her in hopes of glimpsing whatever it was that had claimed her rapt attention.

"Does she need to go out?" Mom wondered.

"No, Mom," Davy said somberly. "Maggie senses the Old Ones are in some kind of trouble. I feel it, too."

A chill crept along his mother's spine. "Really, honey?" she asked. "How can you be sure?"

"I just know," he replied in a tone which conveyed the dejection he felt. "It's why Racer didn't come here this afternoon. If anything ever happens to him...." Davy's voice trailed off as his tears began to well. Mom walked over and stood behind him, placing her hands lovingly on his shoulders. She longed to speak words of encouragement, but they wouldn't come. She hoped her proximity would be comfort enough for now. Maggie stiffened suddenly, and her wet nose twitched in earnest. Without warning, she began barking with wild abandon.

"What's got into that dog?" Jim hollered from the kitchen.

"I don't know, Jim," Mom yelled back, covering her ears to protect them from the raucous noise.

Davy strained his eyes toward the horizon. He thought he saw something moving away in the distance, but could not make out what it was. He blinked away the tears, rubbed his eyes with his shirttail, and stared again. *Yes! There is something coming toward the house and fast! What can it be? Who can it be?* Davy squinted against the shimmering afternoon light and held his breath. *Yes! Yes! It is!*

"Mom, Mom!" he shouted with newfound glee. "It's Prancer! And Racer's riding on his back!" Davy flung open the screen door and flew down the steps, running at full-tilt to meet them. Maggie, though not on his heels, hurried after him as fast as her ancient legs would permit. They rendezvoused where the wild meadow gave way to a manicured lawn. Davy threw his arms around the neck of the winded Prancer while Racer leaped to the boy's shoulder and peppered the top of his head with whiskery kisses. "Where have you been?" Davy asked. I've been so worried! What's happened in The Glade?"

The buck and squirrel regarded their Chosen One with eyes which simultaneously revealed deep love and a deeper consternation. Racer cupped Davy's face in his paws, careful not to allow his claws to leave so much as an imprint. "My child," he said solemnly, "there is no easy way to tell you this, so I'm going to come right out and say it. Reverend is in dire need of your help. We have come to take you to him."

"Me? Help Reverend? How?" Davy couldn't begin to fathom how he could be of any assistance to the sage and gentle owl.

"We'll explain on the way," Prancer told him. "We have lost much time already."

"Yes, child, run and tell your mother that you are needed most desperately," said Racer, bounding from Davy's shoulder onto Prancer's back.

"No!" Maggie barked sternly. "I'll not have it!" She had caught up with them at last, and her remark took them all by surprise. "How can you even think of putting the boy in such danger?"

"Danger?" Davy searched the faces of his friends for confirmation at this startling turn. Neither of them offered to contradict Maggie's declaration.

"Maggie, my dear," Racer said kindly, hoping to calm her. "If there were another choice, by glory, don't you know we'd take it?"

Prancer leaned down to nuzzle the dog's neck. "We'll protect him. You know that," he said consolingly.

"Protect me? Protect me from what?" Davy asked, his voice quavering.

Maggie pulled away from Prancer and placed herself squarely between the Old Ones and the boy. "How can you protect him when Reverend couldn't even protect himself?" she growled. "Answer me that!"

Racer and Prancer exchanged stricken glances. Tears were in the squirrel's eyes as he dismounted once again and stood in front of the old dog whose own eyes were clouded with fear. "Maggie, how long have you known me?"

"Don't be silly, Racer. You know as well as I do that I was a pup when we met."

"And in all those years, did I ever once put Will in a situation I couldn't handle?"

"No, but this is different. Horribly different."

"The circumstances may be different, but not the depth of my care and concern," Racer stated and, gazing at Davy, added, "and my great love for the Chosen One."

"And just how are those things going to save him from the... from the...." Maggie could not bring herself to name the evil she both sensed and smelled as it emanated foully from The Glade.

"Maggie, Maggie," Racer sighed and shook his head, "don't you remember? Love overcomes all things—always has and always will."

She did, of course, recall, but in her agitated state, the dog could say nothing. The squirrel leaned in closer to her and lowered his voice to a whisper that Davy could not hear. "In his lucid moments," Racer told her, "Reverend has cried out for the Chosen One. Davy must come with us and come now. If he doesn't, we may lose Reverend forever. Is that what you want, my dear?"

Maggie hung her head despondently, her mournful eyes reflecting her breaking heart. Racer laid his paw on her silky neck and stroked it tenderly. She longed with all her being to have this dilemma disappear. She did not want to make a choice as grievous as this one, but choose she must. Not trusting her emotions enough to look at the boy, Maggie took a deep breath and said, "Go, Davy. Tell Kate and Jim you must help Reverend."

"Are you sure, Maggie?" Davy asked, not a little confused by this unanticipated reversal of opinion.

"She's sure, Davy!" Racer shouted as he embraced the dog vigorously. "Hurry, my child, *hurry*!"

Davy didn't hesitate. He turned on a dime and dashed for the house. He wasn't surprised to see Mom standing where he had left her, but was genuinely astonished to note that a slightly bent Jim was at her side, leaning on Grandpa Will's hand-carved cane. When he reached the porch, he leapt up the stairs and through the screened door which Mom was propping open for him. "Mom! Jim!" Davy said breathlessly. "I have to go; the Old Ones need me! It's Reverend!"

"What in the world is wrong with him?" Mom asked anxiously.

Davy shook his head. "I'm not sure," he said, "but, Racer says I'm the only one who can help. Please let me go. Prancer says they're running out of time."

"Running out of time?" Jim scowled. "That doesn't sound good."

"No, it does not," Mom agreed emphatically. "Davy, are you sure there's no danger involved, because if there is...."

"Mom, please," Davy entreated, "it doesn't matter if there is or not. I have to go."

Mom turned toward Jim pleadingly. "Kate," he said, "don't you need to check on those brownies in the oven? I've got this." Mom opened her mouth as if to say something, but closed it when she saw the confident sparkle in Jim's green eyes. She bent down to give Davy a quick hug and retreated to the kitchen, tissue in hand.

"Your back," said Davy, "it's better?"

"Still hurts, but at least I can stand up," Jim answered as his expression turned as serious as the boy had ever seen it. "There's some danger involved, isn't there, son?"

Davy's shoulders sagged and he dropped his gaze. He knew he had to tell the truth and, he had to admit, he wasn't feeling too courageous at the moment. Jim rested his free hand on Davy's shoulder. "'Though I walk in the midst of trouble, you preserve my life,'" he quoted.

Davy looked up at his stepfather. "How do you know I'm scared?" he asked, his voice barely audible.

"Danger naturally incites fear in all but the foolish," Jim assured him.

"Are you going to let me go help Reverend?"

"Could I stop you?"

Davy mulled this over for a second or two. "No," he said slowly and deliberately. "I have to help my friend."

"Godspeed then, son," Jim said, giving the boy's shoulder an encouraging pat. "Your friends are waiting for you and, as you said, they are running out of time."

Any apprehension Davy had harbored miraculously vaporized as Jim's words filled his heart. Grinning broadly at his stepfather, Davy bolted out the door to rejoin Racer and Prancer. Jim remained where he was, eyes glued on the boy and his dog, as he could see nothing of the Old Ones, curious as to what would happen next. He saw Davy give Maggie a hug, then watched him throw his right leg over an invisible object near the ground. It looked as if the boy had perched himself on a very small pony. To Jim's amazement, the "pony" stood up, and Davy appeared to be levitating in thin air. "Prancer," Jim whispered as Davy bounded through the meadow, seemingly buoyed by the tall, waving tips of the grasses and wildflowers. He watched until the boy was a mere speck on the horizon, praying all the while. *With your right hand, you save me.*

Chapter 13

Evil in The Glade

Running at top speed to return to his friends, Davy noticed that Prancer was lying down on the grass with Racer perched on his shoulders. The squirrel's wild gesticulations meant to encourage the boy to hurry even faster made him want to laugh out loud in spite of the dire circumstances surrounding them. With a final burst of speed, which surprised even him, Davy reunited with his friends in record time.

"Climb aboard, lad," boomed Prancer. "Train's about to leave the station."

Davy's eyes widened with excitement at this prospect. "You mean I get to ride on your back just like Grandpa Will did?" he asked, incredulous.

"Yes, sir," Prancer confirmed. "Hurry now."

"I love you, Davy," said Maggie forlornly.

"Oh, Maggie," he said, wrapping her in a hug both quick and firm, "I love you, too. Please don't worry. Everything will be okay. I'll hurry back as fast as I can."

"And I'll be right here waiting for you," she promised.

Davy released her reluctantly, but knew time was of the essence. Without further ado, he clambered up on Prancer's back, and the gigantic buck eased himself to his feet, assessing the extra weight. "Scoot up more toward my shoulders. That's a good lad."

For a brief moment, Davy, only once having ridden on a sullen pony led by an equally sullen clown at a carnival, felt giddy at this new height, and surprised by the tautness of Prancer's muscles against his legs. "I won't fall off, will I?" he asked apprehensively.

"Haven't lost one yet, and I don't intend to do so now," Prancer told him firmly.

"He's prayed the Prayer of Claiming," Racer explained from his perch on Prancer's head. At Davy's befuddled expression, he added, "It means you both are one for the time being. Enjoy the ride, child!"

Without so much as a how-de-do, Prancer was off like a shot, bounding through the meadow as if his hooves had springs. Davy lurched slightly and his breath caught in his throat at the sudden takeoff, but it wasn't long before he felt his body synchronize with that of the buck. It was as if he had been riding on deer his entire life. The wind whipped at his face while the grasses and wildflowers lapped at his feet. Davy had never felt such a surge of exhilaration before. He longed to whoop and holler for the sheer joy of it, but the solemnity of their mission deemed it inappropriate.

Davy realized, not without uneasiness, that neither Racer nor Prancer had yet to offer any explanation concerning why Reverend needed his help and, just as puzzling, why, if time was so crucial, were they not using the means of instant transport? The squirrel, balanced between the buck's enormous antlers, had his back to Davy. His tail was flicking nervously as if it had a life of its own, and his shoulders were hunched with what appeared to the boy to be tension. He recalled seeing Mom's shoulders do the same thing when she had driven down the steep and winding road to the farmhouse for the first time. Davy had known better than to speak to his mother when she was in that state, and wondered if he needed to show the same respect to Racer now. He decided to remain silent for the time being and wait, he hoped with the patience he was still trying to cultivate, until the squirrel was ready to elaborate on the details.

To distract himself, Davy paid closer attention to the scenery speeding by them. They had already left the meadow far behind, and Prancer, as though his strength knew no limits, was leaping along an indistinct trail that would lead them to The Glade from the farmhouse's side of the ridge. Jim had informed them just the other day that the trail they had taken to the recent feast hosted by the Old Ones was the only way Grandpa Will had ever walked in order to get there. "I'm sure there are other ways to reach The Glade," Jim had observed, "but they're probably longer and more arduous."

"What does 'arduous' mean?" Anna had asked. Davy, who hadn't known what the word meant either, was relieved when his sister jumped in with the question.

"It means hard or difficult," Jim had answered.

"Then why didn't you just use 'hard' or 'difficult' in the first place?" Anna had wondered.

"Why, Miss Priss, to improve your vocabulary," Jim had said, laughing and tugging on her braid.

Davy realized now that 'arduous' was an apt descriptor for the path Prancer was taking. His speed decreased considerably as he negotiated boulders and fallen trees along the way. The boy could feel the buck's rib cage heaving under the strain, and felt sheepish knowing his own weight was contributing to Prancer's duress. "Are you okay, Prancer? Should I get down and walk?"

"No," the buck grunted, "take...too...long."

"He'll be all right, won't you, Prancer?" Racer asked, gazing ahead from the vantage point of one gargantuan antler upon which he had scrambled. "We're not far from the top, my friend. After that, it's smooth sailing along the ridge to The Glade."

Prancer responded with a resounding wheeze and redoubled his efforts, more determined than ever to gain the ridge where the trail sloped agreeably, and leave this rugged terrain behind him. Racer tumbled from his antler perch and returned deftly to the top of the buck's head. Then, to Davy's wonderment, the squirrel began to sing, his mellifluous voice as clear and as sweet as it had been last Sunday at church. Although he couldn't understand the words, the enchanting notes penetrated his heart and surrounded it with an unquenchable hope. Instantly, he felt refreshed and renewed in spirit as the tune swept beneath him like a wave, buoying him up and carrying him away on a resplendent sea. The song seemed to have the same effect on Prancer, as his gait waxed more strong and sure, and his breathing became less labored. As Racer continued singing, the grueling, uphill ordeal was miraculously transformed. To the buck, it now seemed as effortless as a casual stroll down a wide and well-worn trail, and his energy was burgeoning by the second. "Keep singing, Racer!" Prancer shouted. "Even when we get to the ridge, keep singing!"

"Yes, Racer," Davy laughed merrily, all the worries that awaited him driven far from his heart and mind, "keep singing all the way to The Glade!"

With that, the squirrel threw his head back, eyes closed blissfully, and sang even louder and more melodiously than before. Their hearts and souls were cheered to the very brink of bursting by the time Prancer broke through a last thicket and arrived at the ridge with its broad, welcoming path stretched before them. If Davy thought the buck had coursed the meadow at breakneck speed, he realized it was nothing compared to the pace at which Prancer was hurtling now. His hooves thundered over the ground, which became a veritable blur to the boy. He shut his eyes tightly to keep from getting dizzy.

The wind and the clear, soaring notes of Racer's song rushed into Davy's ears, and his heart pounded jubilantly at the sheer excitement of the ride. He thought the buck could only go faster if he sprouted wings, and he found himself wishing this thrilling journey could last forever; but before Davy could entertain another thought, he realized that Racer, without skipping a beat, was at last singing words he could understand.

They that wait upon the Lord
Will be made strong,
On eagles' wings, they rise,
For Him, they long.
They that wait upon the Lord
Will, unwearied, run
From dawn of day
To setting sun.

It's a prayer! A prayer sung for Prancer! Davy's mind whirled almost as swiftly as the ground beneath him. Unlike the prayers he said, and, too often, neglected to say before bedtime, this one was vibrant with presence and power as though the Lord, Himself, was dashing along right beside them. Davy's eyes flew open and he looked around frantically and expectantly, but all that met his gaze was the trunks of trees approaching and receding with an alarming swiftness. He squeezed his eyes shut again and turned his full attention to Racer's song. The squirrel sang the verse numerous times, and Davy found himself mouthing the words, savoring each one as if it were as sweet and delectable as Mrs. Hopper's blueberry cobbler. An overwhelming sense of peace encompassed him, and Davy knew, though his eyes had revealed nothing, God was with them in that moment.

***

The malodorous smell emanating from Reverend's chambers now permeated the Banquet Hall where Builder and Mrs. Builder, with seemingly inexhaustible energy, were handing out handkerchiefs doused with the refreshing scents of wisteria and lemon verbena. Cleverhands, having returned from a brief nap, gratefully accepted his and promptly draped it over his nose. "What a relief!" he exclaimed. "Thank you, Builder."

"Are you sure our patients aren't affected by this horrendous stink?" Builder asked.

"Don't seem to be," the raccoon replied. "I've asked the ones who are awake, and they don't even know what I'm talking about."

"All the more blessed for them," said the beaver. "They've suffered enough for one day."

"Haven't we all?" Cleverhands sighed. He patted Builder congenially on the back and resumed his rounds.

As he waddled off to make more deliveries, Builder's mind replayed the ghastly scenes of this most unfortunate day. Throughout the countless years, there had been tragedies and calamities that the Old Ones had been called upon to address, but he could not recall there ever having been a day when so much grief and shock and sadness had filled the Sanctuary. He was all but numb with weariness, yet refused to give in to it. There was too much to do and too many to help for him to even think about indulging in his own needs. "Here, Whiskers, Mrs. Whiskers," said Builder, handing the mice petite handkerchiefs just their size, "these should help matters."

"Thank you kindly," Whiskers responded hoarsely, taking both of them in one paw as the other one was wrapped around Mrs. Whiskers' shoulder. She had been the one who had reported Reverend's turn for the worse to the others, and she was still reeling from the whole terrifying ordeal.

Mrs. Whiskers had been returning to her friends, pushing a wheeled cart rife with refreshments. Just as she had entered the room and had been setting out cups for tea, Reverend had emitted an unearthly wail and had begun thrashing around uncontrollably on his pillows. Frightened out of her wits, the mouse had let out a squeal and dropped a cup and saucer where they, she imagined now, must still lie in shattered chaos on the stone floor. Mrs. Whiskers had fled the scene in haste to report the grim news. Upon hearing it, Prancer had dashed to Reverend's chambers, and the other Old Ones had gathered in a large circle to pray in earnest for their dear friend. It had been the mouse's turn to offer prayers when they had heard the clatter of the buck's hooves growing ever closer at a manic speed. He had flown into the Banquet Hall, stopping only long enough for a returned Racer to jump on his back, and had barreled straight toward the Blessed Portal. "Going for help!" Prancer had bellowed as he zoomed past them and disappeared from view.

Now, still shaking inside, Mrs. Whiskers leaned her head upon Whiskers' shoulder. "How long has Prancer been gone?" she asked forlornly.

"Not sure," he answered, "but he's getting help for Reverend, and that's the most important thing."

"But what kind of help, I wonder? Who could possibly...." Mrs. Whiskers stopped mid-sentence. Suddenly she knew who Racer and Prancer had gone to fetch: precious Davy, their Chosen One. Just the mere thought of that poor boy having to see what she had seen broke her heart. She turned to Whiskers, and said in a trembling voice, "It's Davy. It's Davy who will save Reverend."

Whiskers hugged her tightly. "Not without God's help," he said, and the mice held each other closely and prayed with renewed vigor.

***

The three companions were still a quarter-mile away from The Glade when Racer and Prancer began to detect the noxious odor, faint, but growing ever stronger the closer they came. "It is as I told you," the buck shouted to the squirrel. "Can't be good if it's actually escaping the Sanctuary."

Racer made a valiant effort to continue singing in spite of the putrid smell, but it finally got the best of him. By the time they emerged from the shade of the forest into the sparkling sunlight of The Glade, the squirrel was wracked with coughing and trying futilely to shield his nose with his paw; Prancer was snorting miserable, his pace reduced to a listless walk.

"What is it, Racer?" Davy asked in alarm when his friend's song had surrendered to spluttering. "Why have you slowed down, Prancer?"

"Don't you smell it?" Racer said, almost choking on his words.

"Smell what?" Davy sniffed the air with purpose, but his nose revealed nothing out of the ordinary.

"That stench," Prancer gasped and wheezed as he came to a full stop. "Can't...go...on." With that, the gallant buck's legs collapsed beneath him and Davy, with Racer, tumbled off his back, landing in an awkward heap on the cushiony tussocks of grass. Startled, but unhurt, Davy quickly got to his feet and surveyed the plight of his friends with dismay. Both were sprawled listlessly on the ground, their eyes closed as if they were in the deepest of sleeps.

"Racer! Prancer!" Davy cried repeatedly as he nudged, shoved, pushed, and pulled at them in turn, trying in vain to rouse them to consciousness. His heart, which had been so filled with peace and courage just a short time ago, now pounded with panic and fear. *What if I can't wake them? What am I supposed to do?* With tears streaming down his cheeks, Davy redoubled his efforts to revive the buck and the squirrel, but to no avail.

Exhausted and defeated after what seemed like an eternity of effort, Davy sank to his knees on the grass between the two and stared with bleary eyes across The Glade. It was then he noticed the Blessed Portal, glistening in the sunlight, but something seemed amiss. Wiping his eyes hastily, Davy blinked and scrutinized the Blessed Portal again.

Its once scintillating points of light were growing dull, and he perceived, to his horror, specks of black floating and merging around and within them, slowly, yet methodically, absorbing each one.

A dread like nothing Davy had ever known, or could ever have imagined, descended upon him, wrapping him in a vise-like grip. Even though the sun was shining, the boy shivered and quaked as if he was standing barefoot in the snow. Feebly, he tried to get to his feet, but his legs had turned to jelly, and he dropped again to his knees. Although Davy had never watched anyone or anything die, he knew in his heart of hearts that he was witnessing it now. *The Blessed Portal is dying. The Blessed Portal is dying. The Blessed Portal is dying.* He attempted to avert his eyes from the unthinkable spectacle before him, but they were riveted beyond his will, and the words of doom rang dolefully in his ears: *the Old Ones will die. The Old Ones will die, the Old Ones will die...*"

"They can't die, they can't. I won't let them!" Davy shouted defiantly, and with one more heroic attempt, struggled to his feet. No sooner had he attained a wobbly balance when he was struck down mercilessly by an invisible blow to his chest. He lay inert between Racer and Prancer, his head spinning, his lungs heaving as they tried to regain the wind that had been knocked out of them. Davy tried to move his limbs, to raise his head, but his body refused to respond. He was powerlessly affixed to the ground.

"And there you will stay, O Chosen One," hissed the most wretched and malevolent voice he had ever heard. The words carried the horrid odor, surrounding the boy in a nefarious cloud.

"Help!" Davy's mouth formed the silent word, and his world was plunged into darkness.

About the Author

Martha Jane Orlando fell in love with the Nantahala Mountains of North Carolina when her husband, Danny, and she stayed there on their honeymoon.

Martha Jane is a former middle school teacher who has a son and a daughter, and two stepsons, all grown.

Aside from writing fiction, Martha Jane also pens a bi-weekly devotional blog, Meditations of my Heart, which you can visit at marthaorlando.blogspot.com. She has created a fan page which you can visit at gladetrilogy.wix.com/theglade. Your comments and feedback are warmly welcomed!

Martha Jane will be the first to tell you that her passion for writing runs second only to her passionate love for the Lord. She is blessed to help Danny lead contemporary worship each Sunday at their church, Kennesaw United Methodist, in Kennesaw, Georgia, where she resides.

What will become of
Prancer, Racer and Davy?
How will Reverend
and the Sanctuary be saved?

THE ANSWERS COME TO LIGHT
IN THE NEXT INSTALLMENT OF

Adventures in The Glade,
Redemption

AVAILABLE
IN EARLY SPRING, 2015

CPSIA information can be obtained
at www.ICGtesting.com
Printed in the USA
FFOW05n2008011214

9 781939 289537